TIMBO:
THE DARK RADIOGRAPHER

Mulitalo Fiaalii Arasi

Publisher: Inspiring Publishers,
P.O. Box 159, Calwell, ACT Australia 2905
Email: publishaspg@gmail.com
http://www.inspiringpublishers.com

 A catalogue record for this
book is available from the
NATIONAL
LIBRARY   National Library of Australia
OF AUSTRALIA

National Library of Australia The Prepublication Data Service

Author: Mulitalo Fiaalii Arasi
Title: TIMBO: The Dark Radiographer
Genre: Fiction Novel
ISBN: 978-0-6483865-1-3

'No one who achieves success does so without acknowledging the help of others. The wise and confident acknowledge this help with gratitude',

Alfred North Whitehead

Acknowledgement

This book would not have been possible without the encouragement and full support of my family. I have every pride in acknowledging the undying efforts of my children, *Muaimalae, Loimata, Anna, Anne* and *Vala,* in reading and re-reading this book until it becomes as it is. I treasure every constructive comment they voiced in making this project a reality.

My special thanks to my dear wife, *Siulepa*, for her unwavering support that gave me the strength and determination to write this book.

Above all else, thank be to God the father for the strength that keeps me moving and the hope that keeps me believing that the equilibrium of His love is always sustained as revealed in this book.

Cheers.

Table of Contents

Prologue

This book is about a truthful depiction of both sides of the coin in the way we live in our beautiful world, from one extreme to the other. It is revealed through the life of an island boy whose journey was enhanced through the various sponsorships, without which he would not have known the beauty of the other side of the world in culture, beliefs, geography and development, just to mention a few.

Thus it is also an acknowledgement of the lending arms of many kind souls individually, various developed countries, and in particular the UNO and its subsidiaries, to the underdeveloped countries and their marginalized citizens.

The names are all fictitious but the book is based on true events.

May you relish every minute of reading it and join me in thanking those who are trying to make unfortunate lives more meaningful and our world a peaceful and comfortable place to live.

Enjoy.

A New Dawn

It was 9.00 o'clock on a Sunday morning. Timbo was supposed to be at church but he was now waiting for the bus heading to start a new life. It was a new milestone in his life. He was excited to see the capital and his new school but also sad to leave his home and friends behind.

Something had to give; his parents and home or his new school and the capital. His father did not look like he had any second thoughts, but he could see his mother clinging onto her maternal possessiveness through her tears. It was harder for her because she had to stay behind with Timbo's other siblings while he was accompanied by his father to his new home.

This was Timbo's first trip away from home. He still had to cross the sea, catch another bus to get to the capital before taking a taxi to his new home. He thought everything would be easy sailing until he witnessed the power of the sea half way to the other island. The waves were getting higher and higher as the ferry pushed its way into the deep ocean. Instead of helping the ferry ease the burden, they kept hitting her with mighty blows.

The ferry he was travelling on was only twenty meters long and less than ten wide. Limited in space, it only had one cabin – which was the captain's. Everywhere Timbo looked, there were passengers. They were standing, holding onto the ferry's poles or sitting on the square-shaped elevated platforms with a small door on one of the sides. Sailors used these platforms to sneak down to the engine room to check on the ferry's cargo.

The sea was restless; waves becoming wild and merciless. The swaying of the ferry was getting more frequent and angled to such a degree that made

Timbo wonder if it would ever make it through to the next wave. Then came a single dong of the bell from the captain's dock; a sailor came running out and yelled to the standing passengers, *'Do not stand on the chain'.*

When Timbo asked his father what the chain was for, his father explained, the chain was connecting the steering to the inboard rudder to steer the boat. He then heard another dong (or was it a ding this time?) while the waves toyed with the ferry. Again, another sailor came out howling at the passengers standing on the starboard side of the ferry, *'Hey, you lot there, move over to the other side. It's too heavy on this side'.* Without a word or retort, they just moved. They knew their lives were in the sailors' hands.

The sea offered no sympathy. The waves just flowed onto the deck from one side to the other like a warrior dancing in tease in front of a defeated army.

Timbo's hope of seeing the capital started to fade. He was also starting to feel guilty. If anything happened to his father; it would be his entire fault because they were travelling to the mainland to pursue his dream. His father was holding fast to his hand. Timbo could not read his father's expression but he could tell he was worried. His thoughts were probably centered not only on Timbo but also his other children and Timbo's mother especially if their journey was doomed. *'This is the roughest part of the channel. We'll be over it soon',* encouraged his father.

As Timbo was dosing off to sleep, he was awakened by the sudden shudder of the boat. The engine had suddenly stopped. The revolting oil smell of the engine wafted across the boat; smoke was starting to seep through the wooden deck causing sailors to swarm down to the engine room like bees to their beehive.

'The boat is on fire', someone yelled from where the sailors disappeared down under.

'What?' a woman behind Timbo questioned in disbelief.

'The boat is on fire', confirmed another passenger.

'Oh no! And what the hell are the sailors doing? Where is the stupid captain?' she roared. The woman was getting restless and agitated. No one bothered to answer her. They were all watching in fear while the sailors battled to contain the fire.

The crew formed a line from the lower levels to the deck, passing buckets of sea water to contain the fire. By the time the fire was extinguished, passengers were in their tenth prayers.

During this time, the sea showed no mercy. It was Mother Nature at her finest as she intensified the situation by sending more waves onto the deck. While in no way did it help to put the fire out, it at least cleaned the deck. Timbo's father was right – this had to be the roughest part of the crossing.

The ferry was in abeyance and floating aimlessly like a baby's discarded wrapped nappy. Prayers kept evaporating from the oldies on deck hoping to clear the cloud of uncertainty. To Timbo, it probably would not have happened had they travelled on any other day but Sunday; a day he was taught throughout his youth to respect as a sanctified day.

Passengers were panicking. Some were crying and calling for their gods; others calling for their wives or husbands and children like a roll call. No one cared who was listening to each other's grievances. It was a shared moment of fear as there was no guarantee for their safety.

It was then a man in a white coat with no tie began to sing,

> 'A pei se vaitafe le fifilemu
> Pe lutia nei I le sou
> I le olaga nei ou te molimau pea
> E lelei, e lelei le Alii[1].

Timbo knew the hymn and he sang along too. To his surprise, everyone seemed to know the hymn. They were not only singing, but sang it louder than he used to hear. Timbo could not hear his own voice because of the lady behind him; she was the loudest of them all.

Next to Timbo was a young expatriate couple. They too were also singing but in their own language,

> 'When peace like river attendeth my way,
> When sorrows like sea billows river;
> Whatever my lot,
> Thou has taught me to know,
> It is well, it is well, with my soul…', (Ville du Harvey[2]).

---

1   *O le Tusi Pese a le Ekalesia Metotisi i Samoa*, 2014
2   *Ville du Harve* by Horatio G. Spatford, 1873

Timbo was trying hard to hear what the man in a white coat was saying in his prayer when he felt a sudden jerk on the boat. This was followed with a splash of slimy seawater which then covered his face. He tried to blink and clear the water from his eyes thinking someone had actually spat on his face. When he opened his eyes, someone whispered, *'It's a whale'.*

The woman behind Timbo overheard it and again blew her frustration, *'A what? A whale? What is that stupid man praying for when there's more trouble coming?'*

Before anyone could provide an answer, the ferry's engine began spluttering, giving hope the engine was coming back to life. But it was not for long. It died again.

Timbo looked over and the man in white was still praying. *'How can he pray without a tie? Can someone tell him to stop it? God only answers those with a coat and a tie',* scoffed the whining lady. *'That's why the engine is still dead'.*

'Will you shut up?' snapped the well-dressed lady from the other side of the ferry. *'Can't you see the boys are trying their best to save us?'.* She too was frightened but remained stoic. It appeared she could not hold back any longer but got the opening to blow it up through the whining lady. This was not only causing distress across other passengers but she was annoyed that she was not helping the situation.

'Hey, was I even talking to you? And who are you to tell me what do?' The whining lady yelled back. *'Look at you, that's why the ferry is not moving; you are too fat for it'.*

'How dare you say that?' she spitefully repelled as she started to make her way for a physical altercation with the whining lady.

'Hey, are you two stupid? Why don't you sit tight and pray instead of acting like kids?', intervened the sailor.

'Please calm down. Don't panic, we'll be alright', counselled the man without a tie.

To diffuse the situation, nearby passengers offered their soothing reassurances while waiting to see if their prayers would be answered. The chaos abruptly ended. Both ladies were separated allowing time for their tempers to cool down.

Before anyone could utter anything more, the engine thundered again and kept thundering. Expecting a loud applause? Of course yes, there should be, but no; the passengers contained their excitement and relief as they weren't quite sure if it was real. It was only when the boat started moving that the loud applause drowned the splutter of the engine as it came back to life.

The sun did not take her eyes off from what was going on during the whole ordeal but could not do much. She could not even understand why the sea had taken so long to toy with Timbo's ailing vessel. It was like a cat playing with her catch until such time she was ready to devour it callously. However, the sea fell short of that.

It was probably not worth doing it or did not have the right to do it. Whatever the causes of her ferocity, no one knew or wanted to know. But her tossing about of Timbo's vessel was traumatic enough to expose the vociferous faithless.

The sun was about to tuck into her blanket when Timbo's ferry finally pulled up into the pier. It felt like the longest day of his life and one hell of an experience. It was an encounter that would haunt him for years to come.

The experience killed his excitement of seeing the capital and dimmed his enthusiasm for attending his new school. However, he was very grateful that he was with his father.

Timbo's father had been through many of these types of trips before. It was why he remained unperturbed throughout the whole commotion. For many of the passengers, thank God that they had finally made it to the wharf. Everyone seemed to be weary if not hungry after a long unpredictable day. However, they still managed to give a glimpse of a smile when leaving the ferry.

Reflecting back, the ferry was too small and too open to have weathered the storm, but she made it to shore without losing a single life. Timbo turned one last time and saluted her for withstanding the might of the sea and, in particular, their childish inconsiderate frustrations; he still could not believe they had survived the ordeal.

Flashback

Timbo was in the backyard of his new home, relaxing and enjoying his hammock swinging synchronously to the cool breeze of the evening. He was admiring and laughing at the birds fighting over the ripe bunch of bananas. They reminded him of the life he had back on his home island.

He used to share the ripe bananas and the coconut meat with some of his classmates during the lunchbreaks. Unlike the birds devouring selfishly, he and his friends used to enjoy sharing lunches, often laughing and being noisy about it.

Timbo and his friends used to drown the echo of the coconut choppings by mashing with ripe bananas which sparked their laughter most of the time. It was loud enough to momentarily be deafening. Thus, they used to ask *'What? What? What?'* each time someone said something when trying to crunch the coconut slices with their tough teeth. They had to demolish them before expiry of school recess. It depressed him deeply when thinking about his friends. He missed their jokes. But it was this echo that would prompt him to stay focussed and continue on.

Reminiscing, Timbo remembered vividly the hardship his parents faced while trying to fund his and his siblings' education. His father would save up all the collection of cocoa beans and dry coconuts until they all arrived home from the different schools they attended.

It was something they all looked forward to during school holidays. He could still hear one of his brothers singing all the way from their house to the paddock once they were on their way to collecting the produce.

They would either join his song in different voices to make it sound like angels in the paddock, or sing one's own song like callers in a race. He did not realise the significance of having siblings back then, but reflecting on it now made him laugh and feel closer to them. He missed the bond they had.

Their hard work always paid off though. When it was time to sell the produce they would take it in to trade for cash. The only obstacle was that the trader would always say he did not have the cash to pay them immediately for the goods.

This was a very frustrating situation for Timbo and his parents as this occurred numerous times. Timbo's family was reliant on this trade and felt they were being disadvantaged as the trader had all the time in the world to have payment ready before they arrived.

It was the eve of returning to school and they needed that money to pay the tuition fees. Timbo's parents were worried, where else would they get the money to pay for fares and school fees? After all, their products had already been sold and they had yet to receive payment.

There were not many options open to their family to make alternative arrangements. Timbo's mother, the more vocal of his parents could not contain her anger. '*Well, what are you sitting here for?*' she prompted his father. '*They've got all our products now. There's nowhere else to get the money from. You should get back to them and tell them to pay us for our products. We are not asking for credit, they owe us money. There's no time to play games. They should have gone to the bank soon after they received our products*'.

'*Yeah, you are right mum*', Timbo's siblings agreed, not to take side with their mother but to validate their parents' frustration.

Timbo's father did not object. He knew he had to get the money from somewhere for the tuition fees but was weighing up his options. He slowly got up and made his way back to the trader again, unsure of the outcome but determined to make his case. This was not the first time they were caught in such a situation. It happened each time Timbo and his siblings were back on school break; but they persistently persevered and pushed their cases to the trader until he or his wife would finally give in.

When Timbo's father returned, he was given just enough for the bus and ferry fares but the rest would be given at a later time when the trader would go to the bank in town.

'I'm sorry, but this is all I have, just enough for your bus and ferry fares. He said he would pay the rest when he returned from the bank', he apologetically declared. Timbo could see his mother's frustration through her tears but could not do much.

'Ok', Timbo's father told his children *'Make sure you've packed everything you need for school before the bus arrives. Bear in mind the hardships we are going through now. If you really love us, try your best and be successful in school. We do not have any money to support you right through but we pray religiously that some kind soul somewhere will help carry you forth to whatever level you can make it to'.*

Timbo's father encouraged them all, *'Remember, be kind and helpful to anyone who needs your help'.* It was a lesson that Timbo would forever remember as he grew up.

The First Test

While Timbo recalled his past, he could not forget the day he sat his exam for the only Selective Intermediate School in the country. It was hard work, he remembered. But that the days and nights of preparing would pay off he was sure.

Once the exam was completed, the other candidates returned home on paid transport. Timbo braved the scorching heat of the tropical sun by marching home alone like a lost soldier.

As the ute passed him by in front of the graveyard, Timbo heard someone calling to him in a sharp commanding voice. *'Hey, you there, pick up that coconut and bring it over'*. It was from the very obese burly shop owner opposite the road. He looked around to check if he was referring to him or someone else but the man called again, *'You'*.

Timbo picked up the dry coconut and took it to the man in the elevated wooden floored hut. *'Come up the steps and bring it over to me'*, he said smiling. Scared and trembling, Timbo climbed the steps with the coconut. *'Take a seat there son'*, he said in a commanding voice, pointing to the corner facing him.

He sat obediently and waited in wonder what the man's intention would be. *'Is he going to devour me to satisfy his big tummy?'* he pondered.

With a change of tone, he asked, *'Are you alone?'*

'Yes sir', Timbo answered timidly.

'*Where are the rest of the students?*'

'*The school is closed for the selective school exam today; only candidates sitting for the exam are in today*'.

'*So are those the rest of the candidates I saw passing you in that ute?*', he asked.

'*Yes, they paid for it; I didn't*'.

Sympathetically, he added, '*Oh well, that's not the end of the world. It's better to have a tough start that ends well than the other way round. I hope you get through. Have something to eat first before you continue*'.

'*Thank you*'.

Before saying anything further, the shop owner's wife turned up with a hand-woven tray of food. Timbo was surprised at the kindness of this shop owner. He was taken aback by the hospitality shown and he gratefully accepted and ate the food as a token of acknowledgement for the thought. It did not take long before he finished. He had to cut short or he would be too full to continue home.

'*Thank you very much sir for your kindness. It's very much appreciated but I have to continue on in case my parents get worried of my whereabouts*'. As he said it, he was on his feet and ready to return the tray.

'*You're welcome.*' The shop owner said. '*Good luck with your exams*', he said in parting. With a handshake and a wave, Timbo bid farewell to the shop owner and his wife and continued on.

Though it would be another hour's walk home, he felt better after recharging his vitality and the thought that there were some kind souls out there who cared other than his own parents..

Upon arriving home he was shocked to see his mother crying. '*Why are you crying?*' He asked her anxiously.

'*I was worried, all the other candidates were back except you*', she said.

'*I was given a treat by someone on the way home. Remember that man with a shop opposite the graveyard? That was the one who treated me*' Timbo explained.

'*Oh! How nice of him*', she said in a very relieved tone.

'*So how was the exam?*' she asked in a change of subject.

'*I should be alright. But she asked if you have a baby*'.

'*And?*' she eagerly pursued.

'*I lied to her you have one. She almost caught me when she asked if the baby cries a lot but I was quick to think and told her that sometimes she cries other times no*', Timbo confessed.

Timbo's mother's mood quickly changed and she laughed. She said, '*Dad and I were fasting for your exams*'.

'*Thank you*', Timbo acknowledged.

Breaking the fast was not only for Timbo's first test for the selective school but also for surviving the walking distance; a feat his parents would salute Timbo regardless of the exam results.

Backdrop

Timbo was born and brought up in the very distal end of the biggest island of Samoa - Savaii.

Samoa was a colonial country in the South Pacific before acquiring independence in 1962. It has two main islands, with the capital in the smaller one, Upolu.

He had been yearning to visit the capital in the company of his parents, or one of them whenever they had a trip, but was told he had to earn it because it would be unfair for others if granted his wish but not theirs. *'If you do well in school, you'll eventually see the capital',* was the usual answer from either parent each time he begged.

Thus, when selected to sit the exam for the only selective school in the country, Timbo thought this would be the best opportunity to see the capital. He just had to make it in. But there was no guarantee. The competition was very tough. There were only sixty positions for the school and more than a thousand sitting candidates in the whole country.

To Timbo, it would be a miracle if he made it. It was even more doubtful because of the distance and isolation from the capital. No one knew of their existence or any connections to the main office that might offer some light to his dream. It's like diving for a diamond without an oxygen tank in the deep sea – he thought. He was definitely dreaming the impossible. However, the opportunity to sit the exam was a once in a lifetime chance to do something different, just like his dream to see the capital. The fruition of his dream would depend largely on him. He was also banking on the storekeeper's blessing and also his parents' fasting. Or could it be the combination of all?

That really encouraged Timbo stay motivated. He had to wake up early at 5.00am to get ready for school. If he could not be on the main road to school by 6.00am, he would be late. The school started 8.00am every day and it took an hour to get there as Timbo had to walk to and from school.

The same went for all the other students attending the same school from his district. There were others living further from school than him and their noises when passing his house each morning, were sometimes an alarm clock too for him. But his parents never failed a morning to wake him up for school. His father always made time to walk him and his siblings to school when the sun was late to rise. He would only return home when either the sun was up or when Timbo's schoolmates joined them on the way to school.

That was Timbo's routine every day then until the principal called him to his office after the morning assembly. While rubbing his knuckles and waited, he was worried his father would give him a good hiding if he found out that he was called to the principal's office. There was no doubt his father would know because his other siblings were in the same school.

'It's your turn', came the call from the secretary.

The door opened and the principal welcomed him in. Before Timbo took a seat he felt a shockwave running through him when the principal shook his hand and said, 'Congratulations son, you've made it to the selective school'.

With eyes wide opened in shock, he could not help staring at the principal. He could not tell whether or not he was serious, nor did he believe what he was hearing. But the principal continued, 'There are five of you from our school and I'm very proud to be your principal because of your performances. I'm sure your parents will feel the same once they know it.'

Before Timbo could say a word, the principal continued, 'You are now on the schools Graduates' roll for this year and I want you to see the secretary for graduates' final preps before the graduation. Do you have anything to say?'

'*No sir*', was Timbo's timid response.

'*You must be excited. Aren't you?*' he remarked cheerfully.

'*Yes sir*', Timbo stoically responded.

Before Timbo finished, the principal was already on his feet and grabbed Timbo's hand, '*Congratulations again and best of luck*'.

'*Thank you sir*', was Timbo's last words while the principal walked him to the door.

Surprisingly, the secretary was at the door to greet him, '*Congrats. You've done well*' she said.

'*Oh thank you*'.

Before he said anything more, she added, '*This is the list of what to bring on the day of graduation and you have to join the 'Final Year' graduates in their farewell rehearsals after school from now onwards. Come and see me if any problems*'.

'*Thank you*', he could not say anymore. He was still excited and tried to come to terms with such news.

'*You're welcomed and good luck*', were her final words.

Back in Timbo's classroom, word of his success was like a clap of a thunder. While trying desperately to hold his emotions in, he was shocked to be greeted with a loud applause from his classmates upon entering the room. Even more ecstatic was a wink across the room from a classmate whom he adored but was too coy to spit a word of interest to her. And that made his day more than his success story.

On his way home, waves of thoughts bombarded him regarding his success. He was filled with mixed feelings. He was still at a loss whether his success was due to his effort, the shopkeeper's blessing, his parents' fasting or a combination of all.

Whatever it was, his dream of seeing the capital would become a reality. This would mean leaving his parents behind and only seeing them in school breaks. His excitement to see the capital far outweighed all that. He was still too young to have any second thoughts on whether or not there was any other option but to cherish the good news.

Climate Change

Timbo's selective school was not a boarding one. Thus, his dad had to accompany him to his new host family who happened to be his mother's cousin. Timbo had never met them before and now he was to stay with them until the end of term. It was another opening of Timbo's horizons. A new home let alone a new school; it was a lot to take in.

Timbo was not the only student from his island in his new home, there were seven others; all related in blood either to his mother's cousin or the cousin's in laws. All free of charges, no boarding fees. An amazing feat Timbo could not believe until now. He was, and still is, very grateful for such kindness.

For Timbo's guardian, this was not a problem. He genuinely wanted his charges to do well and succeed in their studies. Thus, he kept checking on how they were going and looked over their tasks each night. He was like a field marshal but very supportive.

Timbo had to ask his assistance every so often in his assignments. He was a very helpful home tutor to all of them. But he was sneaky too. He was on their backs all the time. Sometimes, he would pretend to leave home at night during their study time as a decoy for them to assume he was not around and started a 'mouse cat game'. But he would then park his car a short distance away from home and stealthily prowled from outside for anyone not studying and he would really go for that person.

One night he finally caught his prey. Timbo and the rest of the boys were doing their studies when Bob suddenly turned up. After checking on Timbo's assignment, he asked his other cousin, *'What are you doing Eddie?'*

'I'm writing my essay', Eddie replied without knowing that Bob would check on it.

'Can I have a look?' To Bob's surprise, on the very front page of Eddie's alleged essay, it said, *'My Dearest Poor Girl'*. Bob could not contain his emotion but said, *'So this is your essay – **My Dearest Poor Girl?'**.* He read it aloud so all of them could hear the very first line of the supposed essay.

The burst of laughter was instantaneous. No one ever thought of someone writing a love letter during study time. Their laughter was shelved in a tick of a second so as not to annoy Bob even more. *'So what do you mean poor when she's your dearest?'* continued Bob.

Eddie was dumbfounded.

Timbo was trying to hide his sniggering behind his textbook while pretending to concentrate on his studies; he feared Bob might turn his attention to him too. Bob was getting serious with Eddie though, *'Come here, why do you say poor after you said dearest?'* repeated Bob in an angry tone. Eddie did not mumble a word; he was definitely caught off guard then.

'Get up', ordered Bob. Before Eddie was on his feet, *'Dance'*, commanded Bob as he tapped the floor. Eddie had no choice but to dance to the rhythm of the tapping but no music. Because Eddie had a comedic character, he did not care if there was no music but really danced to such an extent that broke Bob's seriousness but laughed gleefully. Wiping off tears of laughter, he said to Eddie, *'You are getting off today. But the next time I find any of you wasting study time, you'll get my hand'*, Bob warned.

After handing back Eddie's book, Bob turned to Timbo and the rest of the boys, in a change of mood and made fun of Eddie's dance. Everyone cracked up laughing as if they never laughed before. Even Eddie countered with more jokes. That was the night to remember in his new home.

1st Door:
The Selective Intermediate School

On the way to school the following morning, Timbo and his cousins could not get over Eddie's romantic debacle. They made fun of him all the way to and from school. They thought it was amusing. Eddie could not care less. He was happy he did not get Bob's 'mighty hand'.

At school, English speaking was compulsory. It was a rule he could not understand why it was implemented when there was only the principal and two other English expatriates in the school. The rest of the teachers and students were all locals. Yet, they would be penalised or even sent home if they spoke their mother tongue. It was a slow process for him because he had to think locally, translate it to English, or vice versa, before he could speak or answer a teacher.

That was the selective school.

His first morning assembly was a disaster. As soon as the principal said, *'Let's pray'*, Timbo could only say, *'Our father.. .'*, and he was lost. He could not keep up with old students' pace. He just could not figure out what the other students were saying until they said, *'...amen'*. He was used to singing the 'Lord's prayer' in his previous school. But he was shocked at the speed the students recited it in this new school. To him, it sounded like the buzzes of bees. For the first few weeks, he just mumbled along to avoid embarrassment until he eventually mastered it.

That was the selective school.

In the previous school, Timbo used to wear a typical uniform of a white short-sleeve shirt and a green strap of clothe wrapped around his hips extending halfway down between the knees and ankles. For the selective school, boys had to wear pink short-sleeve shirts and grey shorts. Timbo felt funny with it. He had never worn shorts before.

Starting school in his first week, he could feel the wind blowing through his thighs upwards. It was an odd feeling and made him constantly check and look again down under whether or not he was wearing anything to school. That was the selective school.

Timbo kept comparing his new school and the old one. Back at home there was never an issue with homework; most of the work was done in school. There never was a threat of being disciplined for not doing it. At his new school, he noted that everything was under the radar. It was either you do it or be sent home or got the parents to see the principal on why the homework was not done. Timbo had to adapt to it, and adapt fast. That was the way of selective school.

Timbo admired the way his principal always dressed smartly in a sharply ironed white shirt and a navy blue short. The principal probably had more than one pairs of white shirts and navy blue shorts. But he was like another student sticking to the same coloured outlook Monday to Friday. Thus, students of other schools used to tease Timbo and his schoolmates as having a principal with 'stingy' pair of pants. Despite that, Timbo still wanted to look smart in uniform like his principal.

One thing Timbo did not realise was that his principal was very observant with eyes like a hawk. One day after school, Timbo and his friends were running across the road without using the crossing; the principal's car drove past at the same time. Unaware of the principal's sharp-sightedness, he was shocked when the principal called out before the end of assembly the following morning, 'Can I see...', and then looked around the assembly until he pointed straight at Timbo and his friends. Not only were they reprimanded, but also put on detention after school for not following rules. That was the selective school.

The Capital

There was so much about selective school for Timbo to absorb. When they had the chance to see the capital with his father Timbo was flabbergasted with shops' facades and the number of cars fighting for every centimeter of the road.

Timbo was strolling with his father along the main street when he heard the chime of the clock once, then twice, and stopped. Timbo looked around to see the source of the sound but his father told him it was the town clock declaring 2 o'clock

Timbo looked and marveled at the structure standing tall in the middle of the capital with its faces blinking every minute in all four directions. Where the sound came from was beyond his wonder. His only experience of a bell in a timely signaling was the priest's church bell back at home informing everyone that someone had kicked the bucket. The number of strikes indicated the age of the deceased; it's an adult if it's more than five but a child if five or less. But this was the chime of the icon of the capital reminding every passer-by the time of the day.

When they flagged the taxi to go home, Timbo's excitement over his first taxi ride was overridden by his struggle in opening the door of the taxi. He had been pulling hard onto the door handle without success. He could have broken the door handle if his father hadn't shown him the small knob adjacent to the main handle to press.

Upon arrival, his father also showed him the silver knob to lift for the door to be opened. Each small wonder was a big eye opening to Timbo.

2nd Door:
The Selective High School

Entering the Selective Intermediate School was one change to Timbo's life. Starting at the Selective High School was another big milestone.

English speaking monitoring though was just as tough as in the Selective Intermediate school. But speaking it was a bit easier this time round than his entry at the Selective Intermediate school. A ruling he still could not get over with as the majority of students and staff were all locals.

There were no more marathon Lord's prayers every morning as used to be or a principal with 'hawk's eyes' that could single out his prey before and after school in public areas.

One interesting change he noted was that they had to move rooms for each subject instead of spending the whole day in one room for all subjects. A change he liked to relieve boredom in the day.

One day a friend sitting next to him pulled the draw of the desk he was sitting on to get some room for his textbooks and saw a lunch packet in it. He whispered Timbo, *'Hey, look!'* Timbo looked and they were ecstatically distracted like blackbirds over a ripe pawpaw. They opened it and there was a chicken sandwich and a chocolate bar.

They exchanged notes under the desk of their move and Timbo's friend suggested sharing the sandwich and giving the teacher the chocolate bar as a leeway out should anything happened. This would be a move they would regret later on. The teacher was thankful for it without knowing the source. While students were busy writing notes from the board, Timbo and his mate could not stop giggling when they saw the teacher enjoying the bar.

The following day, the teacher looked very annoyed. '*Before we start*', he announced, '*I have something to say. Whoever ate the lunch that was in that desk yesterday, stand up now*', was his stern order.

Timbo and his mate were sitting in desks different from the day before. No one could remember who was sitting where on that day excepting Timbo and his friend. They just took whatever desk was available then. No one owned up. The teacher could not believe the indifference of the class. '*Well, if no one owns up, the whole class will stay behind after school to weed the banana patch*', he threatened.

'*But sir*', interrupted the class captain, '*why blaming our class when others were using the same room?*'.

'*That's right*', jumped in others.

'*You were the first to use the room before they returned for the recess and that's when it went missing*', the teacher affirmed.

'*Is it a guy or lady?*' asked Timbo's mate with an expression of anger as if they were a bad bunch.

'*It doesn't matter. All I want is the culprit to own up or the whole class will face the consequences*', he reaffirmed. There was another silence.

The teacher looked around the class and no one appeared suspicious. '*Ok, if no one owns up I will use my magic ruler to find you*', he threatened. No one cared. No one took heed of it seriously either. He started pulling out his ruler from his bag and started spinning it on his finger while students looked on in disbelief until it stopped spinning. '*There you are, the ruler is pointing at you*', referring to Timbo. '*Stand up*', he ordered.

Timbo slowly got up. Before he answered, the teacher asked again with more confidence then, '*Who else? Better own up before I spin again*'.

Timbo's friend slowly got up. '*A Ha! So there you are. What took you so long to own up?*' he asked.

Timbo's friend raised his head and slowly said, '*Sir, we ate the sandwich, and you ate the chocolate bar I gave you*'.

'*Uhhhhhhh*', was the sneering echo from the students. Embarrassed but tolerant, he was like an army general ambushed by his own platoon. He just gave a snaring grin but pride kept his composure. He stood his ground and said, '*Alright, I'll take part of the blame but I want both of you to stay behind after lesson*'.

Trying to deflect students from the embarrassment of the backfire, he quickly opened his book and started writing on the board. '*I want you to copy this as I write*', he stated.

Timbo was not amused but his mate was. It was his mate's initiative that drew Timbo in but now looked as if it was all Timbo's. Timbo was writing as instructed but he was not aware of what he was writing. His mind was all but deflated because of the lunch episode. How tasty was the lunch he could not recall. He no longer cared either. The fact that he could not escape was that he now appeared like an eagle scouring the area for any feed. It really demeaned his thoughts, let alone tarnishing his scholarly record. He only wished that he did not sit next to his mate the day before. His innocence and immaturity would have been still in awe had he sat elsewhere.

The bell went for the end of the period and Timbo started to panic. Though the teacher had the share of the lunch, the onus was still on him and his mate. '*Time's up*', the teacher announced in a firm voice. '*I'll see you tomorrow*'. His anger over the lunch embarrassment seemed to be still haunting him.

Everyone filed out of the door one by one excepting Timbo and his friend.

Timbo's friend was still in a joking mood but Timbo took it seriously. Timbo thought it would have been a bit less of a deal if the teacher was not involved. They would have been let off if it was the lunch only, but embarrassing the teacher was worse. Thus, he was expecting some embarrassing punishment now.

When they had the room to themselves, the teacher raised his head and said, '*Well, look here boys, what you've done was demeaning and embarrassing to you, your parents, your classmates, and in particular, to me. Had you only done it between you, I would not take it seriously. But the way you did it you thought you were smarter than me',* he told them off.

Timbo thought they would be let off but the teacher continued, *'You are senior students and should be role models to the juniors. I want you to take this note to Mr Taylor and don't do it again',* he concluded. The teacher did not sound serious but sending them with a note was enough to tell them how upset he was.

Mr Taylor was a tall very senior teacher in his late fifties with a lanky physique. He always wore his reading glasses halfway down his face. Students called him the executor of the school. He always kept the 'school belt' in his draw. Anyone sent to him during school hours was destined to be in terrible trouble. Thus, Timbo was not amused when sent there.

Mr Taylor had no mercy but did his duty loyally. Soon after Timbo presented him with the note, he devotedly drew the 'school belt' from his top draw and called them one by one.

'Well I have no choice but I don't know when you kids will ever learn', he responded in his usual very high pitched tone.

When Timbo saw there was no student around he quickly stepped forward first and tried to absorb the might of the belt. The first whack was excruciatingly intolerable. He tried to absorb the second one until his bum got numb with the last beating. He did not wait for his friend after taking the last belt but went to the library instead to cool himself. He could not believe being belted at such an age. He was never belted at home regardless of the problem.

That was the selective high school.

Throwing the First Rock

When the school decided to build a Tennis court and a Traditional Cultural Meeting House, they did not have the funds to do so. Thus, they strategised on a project that would raise the funds without impacting the school's budget or affecting parents' support too much.

They began by asking students to volunteer in clearing the school's untouched backyard to grow bananas to be sold.

The school also had a small cattle farm. Each Saturday the students worked on the backyard, a cattle would be killed and each one would be given a piece of steak to take home as a token of thanks for their work.

This went on for a few weeks until the whole field was cleared and then followed by planting of shoots. It was only when the bananas started to bear fruits that the project started to move to the next phase. Once the fund started trickling in, construction of the tennis court began. This was followed with the erection of the cultural and traditional building meant to be used for teaching of local culture and traditions.

When the main central pillar was erected for the cultural and traditional house, Timbo's history teacher, who was also the principal of the school, held the class back after school to say, '*Today, I want you to start filling the new house foundation with rocks*', he declared.

'*Oh no*', rebuffed everyone. '*Why us?*' they openly countered. He tried to be very diplomatic and reason it out with them,

'*Look, you should be proud you'd be the first to throw the rocks for the foundation of this house*', encouraged the teacher. '*It will only be for half an hour, but I want you, my class, to be the first to throw the first rocks for the house. One day in the future when you go past this school, you will be proud to tell your kids you were the first to throw the rocks for this house*'.

The mood amongst students was all but repulsive. No one wanted to know or respond to him.

'*Don't forget*', he emphasised, '*this school was founded by our former Heads of State to meet Foreign Aid criteria for a selective High School[3]. They ignored their statuses but braved the sun in bare feet to trek into the thick bush to size up the location for a school that would groom you to be better educated citizens and be good leaders of the country in the future. This will be your share of thanks for their vision and sacrifice*'.

The commotion subsided even though it did not sink in well especially after school when everyone was dying for food. Rocks had to be carried on shoulders from the newly grown banana patch to the new foundation, each trek with the rocks taking fifteen long minutes. The students then decided

---

3   'Lauga Iupeli Siliva Kolisi o Samoa, 1978' (TuiAtua Tupua Tamasese).

to go together in a line for their principal to see once they all had a rock each. To the principal's amusement, they were not only in one line to the new house but also singing the Beatle's Lyric, *'All we are saying is give peace a chance'.*

He leaned out his office window, smiling and applauded them as they passed him. After their second round, he was already at the foundation site waiting for them. He congratulated them for the effort and thanked them for honouring his word.

'Now you can go and tell your parents, friends and even your kids in the future that you were the first to throw the rocks in filling this foundation. I don't care if you will do it again in days to come but I'm very proud with you and the way you executed my plea. You should be proud too, shouldn't you?' he asked. But to his amusement the boys rebuffed humourously, *'Noooooooooo'.*

They all cheered and so was the principal.

He went on to say cheerfully, *'Many thanks for respecting my word. I'll see you tomorrow'.* They gave him a round of applause as if he won an election campaign. Upon dismissal, they were all in high spirits after hearing his compliments and were as happy as he was.

Undoubtedly, once the building was completed, it became a tangible mark to treasure for years to come. For Timbo and his classmates, it became something to be proud of whenever they would pass it.

The building became a landmark for the students. It symbolised a struggle from nothing to something for the sake of future generations. It was a challenge and reminder for them not to depend more on what's given on the plate, but to consider resources available on hand and to apply a little strategic planning to achieve whatever was in the agenda.

The Local Remedy

Timbo's school was not only underfunded for essential facilities but also understaffed. To fill this gap, there were a number of voluntary teachers from overseas voluntary agencies like the Commonwealth voluntary Service Abroad, and the American Peace Corp Voluntary Program, just to mention a few.

One of them, a slim young lady with contact lenses, was their mathematical teacher. She was soft spoken but smart. Timbo's classmate, Ted, used to overlook her softness and made fun of her to such a point where she could hold on no more but walked out of the class and refused to return unless something was done to him. His classmates were getting frustrated too. They were in their final year where their final results would determine their future but was being jeopardized by Ted's immature behaviour.

Ted was not aware that his future was seriously on the line as well. His actions were meant merely to amuse the class but had reached the point of rejection not only by his classmates but also the school staff. Thus, when he tried to make fun of Timbo before their teacher arrived, Timbo fired back and a fight broke out. Luckily the rest of the classmates joined in to settle it.

When the teacher arrived, everyone was trying to read something as if nothing had happened.

'Well what's happened? It's the first time I find you quiet upon arrival', she wondered cheerily. *'Ted's probably away for being quiet'*, she continued facetiously. But when she looked around the room, Ted was sitting in the corner. When she greeted him, she was surprised to see his upper lip swollen like an apple. In a change of attitude, she called him, *'Are you alright Ted?'*

He did not say a thing but just nodded. *'What happened?'* she wondered inquisitively.

Ted just raised his head and forced himself to say, *'It's just an insect bite'*.

'Do you want to see the nurse?' she asked in a more concerned tone.

'No thanks', he mumbled back.

'Ok, let's start', she resumed.

After the class, Timbo went up to Ted and apologised for the incidence. Moreover, he thanked Ted for not disclosing the incident or they would both be sent to see the principal or even sent home because of breaking the *'No fighting'* school rule.

Ted accepted it and admitted it was his fault. Ted knew also that if he revealed it, that could be the loophole the principal and staff would use to expel him from the school. He had been warned so many times for misbehaving and any minor deviation would definitely see him out of the school gate. Timbo was relieved to know it.

The class did not know it either until they had a session with Mr Lau, the local teacher with a chiefly title. He was specially recruited to teach 'Local Traditions and Culture' for the school. According to him, the principal and staff were seriously vacillating between suspension and expulsion for Ted for any future infractions.

Mr Lau told Ted and the rest of the class, *'I specifically requested the principal and staff to give me a chance to apply traditional and cultural remedies to help 'prune' you again my son, so you can grow to be a smart scholar'.* He went on to say, *'They have already made their decision and been waiting for any incidence, involving you, regardless of who the cause is, minor or major, that would be your exit point. But if you can take heed of my plea and my advice today, you will not only be ignored on that radar, but the principal and teachers will also be more than happy to groom you to be a star for tomorrow not only for the school but also your parents and family'.*

Ted appeared to have heard Mr Lau's counselling. He was in tears; so were most of the classmates. *'Are you crying in remorse or is it because I've told you off in front of the class?'* Mr Lau asked Ted.

'I'm sorry, Mr Lau. I really appreciate your kind consideration for me. I promise I won't do it again', apologized Ted.

'Are you sure?', reaffirmed Mr Lau.

'Yes Sir', assured Ted. He turned to the class, *'I'm sorry mates'.*

Mr Lau got up and shook Ted's hand and patted him on the back. *'I'll take your word for it',* he reassured Ted. They both turned to the class and consoled each one. The class applauded the goodwill gesture displayed.

Timbo reckoned Mr Lau had scored a point. It was just a matter of time to observe the truthfulness of such a pledge.

The Excursion

While rewinding his mental clock to review some of the hard times he faced at high school, Timbo remembered the day they were studying the chemical process involved in the making of soap. It coincided with the opening of the new and only soap factory in his country.

After the lecture, Timbo's whole class was invited to visit the soap factory to view first-hand the chemical process on a large commercial scale. Timbo and classmates were very excited as this was the first time they would ever visit a manufacturing factory.

The school teacher overseeing the excursion was a recruit under the Commonwealth Voluntary Service Abroad program. She was a joyful lady with a Ph.D. in Chemistry. Timbo and his classmates remembered her for her smiling face whenever she talked about the laughing gas. They had not seen her in any other mood.

During the visit, Timbo and his classmates were very impressed with the process. Likewise the teacher was commended for the students' good behaviour during the whole visit. Thus, the company happily donated a full box of bar soaps as a token of appreciation for the students' courtesy.

This was presented in the bus. The teacher acknowledged it on behalf of the students. Excited with such an award, she offered them to help themselves in the presence of the boss. She might have thought it was a good idea to give them while the manager looked on. However, it turned out to be her biggest mistake. She did not foresee the other side of the coin. It was then that everything turned upside down.

To the teacher's horror, it was like a school of cubs fighting uncontrollably over their feed. Students were fighting for more than one bar of soap. She had to shout to the top of her voice twice to bring the students under control. They thought it was a joke but the teacher was furious. She was red in the face looking like a lion ready for a kill. She never expected this. She forgot the students were all from low income families and getting something free was like the end of the world.

Thus, students fought for more than one, not as a souvenir but for the sake of their families. She was so annoyed that she ordered all bars back into the box to be returned with an utmost apology.

'*Why the hell is she doing this when it's not hers?*' complained Timbo's friend in a low irate whisper.

'*True. She's probably after the boss*', giggled Timbo.

After all bars had been returned, she turned to the students, *'I'll see you back in school'.*

'Who wants to see her again?', retorted Timbo's friend, as the bus made its way back to school.

The atmosphere was gloomy all of a sudden in the bus. From a jovial beginning to a dismal ending; no one wanted to talk about what happened. All they wanted then was for the bus to speed up in order to arrive at school quickly and vanish from school before seeing the teacher again. They could not though they agreed; they had to wait for her.

As expected, the teacher blew up again upon arrival. After dismissal, Timbo's friend whispered, *'I don't know why she kept going when she's taken the soaps back'*, he complained.

'Very true, we probably have killed her chances of advancement with the boss', Timbo added humorously before they parted.

'I'll see you tomorrow', his friend bid farewell

'Yeah, don't forget to have a shower even without soap', joked Timbo as they parted.

3rd Door: The Scholarship

Timbo was brought up in a country divided by colonial interventions. Families were broken and visitations to neighbouring island nations were subjected to regulations and colonial approval despite speaking the same language and same bloodline. Curfews were imposed especially at night to avoid any unwanted 'enemy' intrusion.

Citizens were forced to work the land to pay tax for the government. Hence, it started resentment amongst the locals. It upset the harmony and peace they used to enjoy. It was even more hurtful when their voices were not heard or consulted with amongst all these changes. Thus, a movement, *The Mau Movement*[4], emerged to counter such impositions to regain their freedom.

Timbo was born a decade before his country gained independence from colonial powers. Though colonial powers had left, there were still ruling residues he had to absorb like night curfews and regulated visitations to his relatives living half an hour's flight away from his home. There were few people working in town. Most of them lived on subsistence farming.

There was not one mine in his country; agriculture was the main source of income. Thus, Timbo's parents had to till the land hard to get him and his siblings somewhere. They earned just enough to cater for school

4   MAU: Samoa's Struggle for Freedom (Field, M. 2008).

fees and uniforms only. Any further advancement to tertiary education was a mission impossible for his dad.

The only avenue that could bring such dreams into reality was to get sponsored by some kind-hearted soul individually, the developed countries or institutes like the United Nations Organisation (UNO) and its subsidiaries. Timbo was aware of this and thus, continued to study extra hard for it.

The scholarships offered by the various organisations did not necessarily match a student's interests but areas that the sponsors and Timbo's government thought appropriate for the future development of the country especially along the science areas

When Timbo started high school, one of his cousins advised him to choose science subjects as most of the scholarships offered were mainly science related. But Timbo really wanted to be a pilot so he could see the other side of the world. Thus, came the year when he was allowed to elect his subjects, he decided to take his cousin's advice and chose all science subjects plus English because it was compulsory.

His gamble paid off. After finishing high school, Timbo went back to his village to spend time with his parents while awaiting the outcome of the scholarship interview. There were no telephones then; landlines or mobiles were non-existent. The only means of communication was the government sponsored radio.

Timbo was relying on the radio for news of his interview and outside news. But on the night of announcement, their radio reception was chaotic. They could only hear funny sounds like a maritime radio battered by the rough sea waves. Thus, their eagerness to know Timbo's destiny that night was all but dashed.

No one in Timbo's household was aware of what the announcement was until Timbo's father returned home from a village meeting the following morning. His father could not hide his excitement. As soon as he sat down he announced it straightaway, *'Timbo's made it; it was announced last night'.*

Timbo's mother was quick to quiet him, *'Are you sure? Why don't you wait until Timbo confirms it instead of spitting it out unconfirmed?'* she cautioned him.

'*Well, everyone in the meeting was talking about it*', he countered. '*In fact that was the main topic of the meeting. So how can I be mistaken?*', his father assured proudly.

'*Better wait for tonight if it be announced again then blow it. Otherwise our son will be like a laughing stock wherever he goes*', she advised. Timbo's father did not counter anymore; he appeared upset at his wife's meltdown. Without another word, he got up again and went to the farm.

Timbo was left uneasy. He felt sorry for the diffusion of his father's excitement. At the same time, he did not want to be hailed a '*wanna be*' in his village.

Night fell and rain drizzled slickly to cool the night. Radio reception seemed to synchronise with the weather. Timbo's father was listening intently for any repeat of the announcement; his mother was not far away with her back to them but also lending an ear.

Timbo's house was an open air one. Any minor whiz of the breeze could distract anyone, but not this time. It was quiet like a place under curfew.

'*This is the list of those awarded scholarships for further studies overseas*', came the announcement. The radio announcement was loud and clear. As soon as Timbo's name was read out, a thundering cheering broke the silence.

'*YEEEEEEHY, Dad was right*', Timbo's sisters hailed. His father applauded it more with a loud clapping. His mother swiftly turned around with a big smile and joined her husband's applause.

Everyone in the house cheered as if they had won a lottery. Timbo returned an acknowledging smile to them all. He had finally made it. He had won a favour for his parents; a payoff for the sacrifices they made for them all. He would be the first of his siblings, family, and village to go on a scholarship to study overseas. This was another door opened for Timbo.

Timbo tried to play it down, but his father could not contain his excitement. He was over the ninth cloud. Whenever he met a friend, he would always try to steer the conversation to Timbo's achievement and why not? He deserved to be commended for his unflagging effort in the land to fund their studies. It was an achievement worth acclaimed.

Timbo did not have a good sleep that night. While he was elated with the news of his award, he needed time to process what this meant and time to farewell his dreams of being a pilot. Despite that, Timbo was very grateful to the countries and institutions that were kind enough to offer them the opportunities to continue their studies.

Life on Campus

Taming the Drumstick

Leaving home and arriving in a new country to continue his studies was a big step for Timbo. So much of the unknown lay ahead and now the support of his family was limited to letters and infrequent visits. It suddenly dawned on him what a big step this was. Excited and a little nervous, Timbo decided to be open minded about what this new chapter could offer.

When he arrived at University of the South Pacific, Suva, Fiji, on his first night, there was a lot of excitement amongst the old students with the new arrivals. Timbo was amazed at how different ethnic groups welcomed and treated him and the other new arrivals as if they had all met before. He was even more impressed when he heard them speaking each other's language, especially the swear words, not in an offensive intention but as a greeting in tease.

The vociferousness continued for a while until the food was ready. To Timbo's surprise, the table was fully set with knives and forks and spoons, a culture he had not fully committed to utilise at home. Thus, he was a bit hesitant in starting.

Back home, Timbo's life at home and with his host family in town was simple. He would either use a spoon or a folk but not a knife and a fork as common to western families for meals.

Others started eating soon after receiving their dinner but he was still joking and laughing with the current students. It was not because the jokes were really funny but he used them as a ploy to observe how to use the knife and fork. It was only when there was hardly anyone talking that he started devouring his dinner.

He was very cautious in ascertaining he was doing the right thing. Unfortunately the drumstick did not seem to allay his inexperience. It kept slipping from his fork like a pet trying to jump out of the fence. Thus he was laughing at each minor joke to release his frustration over taming the drumstick with the knife and fork.

Once he saw one of his new friends using his hands to hold his drumstick, he decided to follow suit. No one seemed to care at the way they ate which was a relief to Timbo. They were all demolishing theirs ravenously after a long trip.

It was Timbo's first taste of the western lifestyle. He had to learn and learn fast. The night ended swiftly. With all the things he was there to learn, Timbo never thought it might also include a knife and a fork. Funny that but that was uni life.

The First Dance

It was a first experience for Timbo to be part of a multiracial social night; the *Orientation Dance* to welcome new students. While in his late teens, he had never seen such a unique scene of students from different ethnic backgrounds mingling and enjoying a social night together.

However, despite such enjoyment, he noted that it was a bit of a struggle to find someone to dance with because of the size of the hall. It was even harder with the segregation seating. It was not because of any pre-arranged order but because this was the students' first experience with such a festivity; a fete comparable to a sports arena where supporters sit in teams and observe each other.

The dancing hall was massive. Each time Timbo started to make a move toward a lady for a dance, someone had already cut in front of him because of the distance he was sitting. Getting a dancing partners was becoming more than a joke. He noted that some smart guys could beat the distance problem by bowing from where they were standing as long as the lady could see them. He thought he'd better try the same, and it worked.

Timbo noted a smooth looking local lady in yellow looking at him most of the time. As soon as the band started to play he shot up and bowed straightaway without moving a step. It seemed she'd been waiting for Timbo to make the move. She walked straight to meet him halfway down the hall and off they swayed to the music. With a big sigh of excitement, he finally took to the floor.

Nothing could explain Timbo's feelings especially the warmth of caressing her breasts against him. He could feel his chemistry starting to pulsate. The girl must have sensed it too; she hugged him tighter and rubbed her body against his. He felt her cheeks against his and a swipe of her lips over his as she moved her head to his other side as an invitation for the rest of the night. But it did not last long. The music stopped abruptly and there was uproar of laughter and screaming.

Timbo threw his head backward to someone's loud claim during the loud music, *'SO YOU LOVE ME?'*. Those hearing it screamed cheerily for it. Others called to the band, *'MORE, MORE, MORE…'*, Slowly everyone joined the chorus until the band blasted again. Timbo did not waste a minute. He turned to her again and hugged her even tighter this time as if they had been together for ages.

To his surprise, someone tapped his back. Despite his intention to enjoy the music more with her, he had to let go of her for him out of courtesy. He did not know his mates were watching. After the music, his mates told him off, *'Why did you give away your partner?. Are you chicken?'*, blasted one of his mates.

'Its ok, others are doing the same', Timbo tried to calm them down.

'No Timbo, it's not ok. You do not understand', intervened his other senior mate. *'This is not the first time that guy has done this. He knew what he was doing. He wants to threaten new comers. And that's why you're wrong. Don't be stupid or be scared'*, ordered his mate.

Timbo's anxiety rating plummeted all of a sudden. He was starting to feel different; from a passive peace making person he was groomed to be, to a newly induced aggressive one. A change he did not want to know. But this was uni. He either listened to his mates or be a punching bag for others.

When the next slow music started, Timbo quickly scanned the room for the same lady and there she was eyeing him from the corner like a cat lying in bay for her catch. He shot up again and bowed to her from his standing distance. Again they were swinging aimlessly to the sweetness of the music. Timbo did not want to step too much to avoid his untrained feet from stepping on her toes. He could feel the same on her; she was digging her head into his chest as if she had just found her comfort zone.

Much to Timbo's annoyance, just as they were just in rhythm with the music, he felt a tap on his back again. Upon turning his head, it was the same guy who tapped him before. His mates were correct. This guy was looking for trouble. Before he let go of her, someone grabbed his collar from behind. Commotion started.

He could not see who was fighting who. It was like a free for all battlefield; each soldier for himself. Timbo did not want to let go of his partner but he had to for his sake; he had to fend for himself. The music was getting louder and faster as if in resonance with the commotion but it meant nothing to anyone. Timbo had never fought before but his reflex to the challenge was like a new boxing star was born.

He did not want to be a chicken as his mates labelled him. He had to prove himself to his mates and most importantly, his dancing partner. He felt his arms locked from behind after knocking his opponent to the ground. He was sweating profusely and puffing like he had just finished a relay. While trying furiously to free himself, he recognised one of his mates' voice calling, *'That's enough'*. He felt his arms released; they were his mates. *'That's enough'*, repeated his mate. *'It's good you listened'*.

The band stopped; the dance floor was empty. Lights were brightened again. Most had left the venue while the senior members of rival groups were trying to resolve the chaos. Timbo wanted to vanish straightaway. He could not believe such a night; from a very cool welcoming start to a very vitriolic nonsensical end.

He was ashamed of his actions. He was also worried of the aftermath that he might be sent home. That would be very embarrassing to his parents. His village people would talk at home that he failed the course before getting the right gospel. What an introduction to uni for Timbo but that night stayed with him a long time.

The Disastrous Date

When Timbo woke up the following morning, he reassessed his actions from the previous night. It was ugly he reflected. Most important of all was that his romantic prospective in campus had plummeted below zero. Thus, when meeting the same lady he danced with at the bus stop the following Saturday, he could not stand the thought of confronting her.

Timbo tried desperately to dodge her but to his surprise, she walked over to him, *'Hi, remember me?'*, she tried to break the ice. *'I'm the one you danced with before the chaos in the orientation dance'*, she continued before Timbo said a thing.

'You look different. I did not recognise you', he pretended to say as he admired her. *'I'm sorry about that night'*, he apologised.

'Oh no no, it's not your fault, its mine', she sacrificed herself.

'Please no. I take full responsibility for my stupidity', Timbo diplomatically offered.

Before he said anymore, she quickly cut in and introduced herself personally, *'I'm Janet anyway. I'm taking sociology. How about you?'*.

'I'm Timbo'.

'That's a nice name'.

'Thank you'.

'What are you doing?'

'I'm here to study Medical Science'.

'Medical What?'.

'Medical Science'.

'That sounds very challenging. Aren't you scared of blood?'

Embarrassed and feeling offended he forced himself to say, *'No, not at the moment but maybe sometimes in the duration of the course'*.

'Wow! That sounds very interesting. Maybe you can teach me more about it someday'.

Timbo was not quite sure whether she really meant it or was she just starting to warm up with him. He was awestruck with her attitude; she was very open with him.

Timbo was always slow in conversation. His problem was that English was his second language. Even though he understood and spoke it, he often had to mentally translate his thoughts into English first before he spoke or vice versa when spoken to. It was then that he had just realized the importance of the 'English speaking rule' he used to criticize back at home in the Selective schools.

Janet was always leading the conversation. When the bus stopped she was quick to offer to pay for their fares. Timbo was not only slow in reaching for his pocket but also had to show his courtesy by letting her in to the bus first. She took the empty seat and offered him the seat next to her. Timbo could not believe whether it was luck or mere coincidence. She took his hand on her lap and poor Timbo was not quite sure what to do; he just tried to relax and follow her lead.

He finally had the courage to start the conversation again, *'I'm going to the movie. Do you want to join me?'* he invited her.

'That's very nice of you', she quickly responded. *'What time?'* she asked.

'The 8.00 o'clock session', he anxiously replied.

'Oh. I would love to if it's the late one because I have to do some shopping first for my Auntie's birthday'.

'That can be done. The same movie will be screened again then', he quickly changed his mind.

'Are you sure? I don't want to spoil your night', she tried discreetly.

'Oh! no, none at all. That will be even better. You've been very understanding. My night will be empty if I go without you'.

'Thank you. What are you going do before then?', she wondered.

'I'll just check the tailor if my clothes are ready and will meet you at the cinema then if that's ok'.

'Lovely, I won't be long dear'.

She quickly swiped a quick goodbye kiss before she disappeared around the corner. Her last addressing of him *'dear'* totally swept him off. No one had ever said anything like that to him nor was he attracted to anyone before. He was so overwhelmed with the speed with which his social life had turned into.

Timbo slowly meandered up to the cinema while trying to come to terms with such sequence of events. His head was all but blown by Janet's charm. It blurred his vision over the glitter of displayed ornaments, while window shopping. She definitely had pulled the fulcrum that kept his mental balance.

While lost in daydreaming for Janet, he unexpectedly stepped on an old sleeping busker's feet.

'OUCH! MY FOOT. OH NO. MY FOOT', squealed the busker. Her scream was like an emergency alarm that attracted a mob of locals in the vicinity; some to help, others in curiosity. He was not quite sure whether to run for his life or attend to her and face the consequences. He took the latter.

Timbo bent down to the busker, *'I'm sorry dear. I'm very, very sorry,'* he apologised while trying to stroke her foot. He was not quite sure if she was in real agony, or blew it to attract attention. She mumbled something in return but he could not understand it.

'What happened?', a firm bass voice inquired from a distance and walking towards her. Before looking up he could tell it was the police officer by slowly scanning his boots upward.

'I accidentally stepped on her feet', he answered back while still massaging her feet to appease her.

'How can you do that to someone as old as your grandmother?' growled the officer. '

'I'm sorry sir, but I did not see her' Timbo explained.

'Oh come on! How can you not see her under the bright light like this? Are you telling me you walk with your eyes on the back of your head? Get up', he ordered Timbo. The cop exchanged words with the lady in their dialect before he led Timbo to the police van.

'Come with me son', ordered the officer.

'Oh no, not again', he retorted mentally. He never thought this would lead to a police involvement. He was in the wrong place at the wrong time. The interview continued at the police van.

'*Do you have any ID?*', queried the officer.

Timbo did not say a thing other than producing his uni ID.

'*A HA! So you're a uni student?*', scoffed the officer. '*It's typical behaviour from you uni guys. You think that just because you are in uni then you can get away with anything you do. Isn't that so?*' asked the officer.

'*No sir*', Timbo replied in a remorseful voice

'*Where are you from?*', asked the officer.

Timbo muttered his birth country.

'*Did you take any alcohol?*' the officer kept pressing.

'*No sir*',

'*Ok, put this between your lips and start blowing until I tell you to stop*', ordered the officer. Timbo did as instructed until the machine gave a whistling sound.

'*Stop now*', the officer stopped him. Timbo saw no reading on the machine's scale.

'*Any drugs?*' the officer continued his investigative stance.

'*No sir*'.

The officer produced a wooden stalk-like piece of material with a cotton wool at its end and gave it to Timbo, '*Take this and scrape the inside of mouth*', instructed the officer. He put it into the scanner for testing and searched Timbo's clothing while waiting for the machine to stop. Nothing appeared on the officer's scanner.

'*I'll let you off this time since you are new here and not familiar with the environment. But watch your step the next time*', warned the officer.

Timbo almost shouted his gratefulness, '*Thank you. Thank you sir*'.

He refrained from the van and continued to the cinema. He was grateful that he was not with Janet during the incidence. It would have indicated to her that he was definitely not as cool as she might think. He glanced at his watch, time had passed so quickly. It was 11.15p.m already and now had to power walk to the cinema in case he missed her.

He was about ten meters away from the cinema when he got a glimpse of her disappearing round the corner and crossing the road to the bus depot.

Janet, Janet, he called while running to catch up with her. She kept walking as if she couldnt hear anything. When he caught up with her, *Janet, it's me*, he begged her.

He was not aware of anything wrong with her until she turned around, *I've been waiting since 11.00 as you promised*, she cried. *I was embarrassed and scared of people making comments at me while waiting. What do you think of me?* she complained.

Timbo was speechless. It was the first time he had to deal with a lady in distress and had no idea what to do. Should he drop to his feet and offer an apology or let her be on her way? He was caught off guard until Janet stopped and leaned against the pillar in front of her. She did not say a word but wiped her tears.

She turned to Timbo, *I'm sorry but I don't think I can make it tonight, may be some other night*. Timbo noted she was obviously upset. However, he was compelled to say something when she said '*maybe some other night*'.

Timbo was quick to apologise once he had her attention. *I'm very sorry dear. I did not mean to hurt you or keep you waiting but I had some trouble on the way to the cinema. That held me down*', Timbo admitted in a very low rueful voice. He had no other excuse but be honest with her if it could change her mind. *I'm very, very sorry*', he continued apologetically. He could only hope madly she would change her mind. As he moved closer to her she was neither receptive nor resentful. She too was trying to conform to her normal self. She was lost as well. This was her first date in uni and not quite sure whether or not she had rushed into it at dawn of time.

Looking at his watch, Timbo realised that they could not make it to the last movie; it had already started. So his night was shattered. But he would rather be happier with a convalescing Janet than trying to make it to the movie. Janet felt it too. It was a disastrous night for both of them. She had missed her aunty's birthday because of Timbo; nothing seemed to be working. It made her wonder if Timbo was really for her or was there someone else better than him.

Her thoughts for her mum before she left her had suddenly hit her. Her mother distinctly impressed on her that her first love was always the best.

Thus, she was in total disarray and confusion. It was their first accidental date but did not seem to work in their favour. She eventually turned to him, *'I'm sorry. I ruined your evening. I should have let you do your things'*, she tried to justify her unwanted behaviour.

Timbo on the other hand was quick to absolve her reaction, *'You shouldn't say that, dear. Maybe it's not meant to be tonight. There's always another day'*, he surrendered. At the same time he pulled out his hankie and wiped her face. She did not resist but let him did his deed. She finally took his hand with the hankie and drew him closer and sobbed uncontrollably over his shoulder as she tried to apologise for spoiling his night. Likewise, he reciprocated in a more comforting slant. They were warming up to canoodling each other when someone asked, *'Excuse me, do you have a lighter?'*.

Surprised at the sudden appearance from nowhere, he quickly turned and answered, *'Sorry, I don't smoke'*.

Before Timbo could ask the intruder where he'd come from, another one appeared from the darkness, and another, and then another. Timbo started sensing trouble. He was more concerned for the safety of Janet now it's very late into the night.

All of a sudden they were surrounded by a group of locals. Janet bravely said something to them in their dialect and thus no one made any move but slowly dispersed again. She was quick to see an oncoming taxi, flagged it down and unreservedly dragged him into it before the local platoon regrouped for a different motive.

'Thanks, you saved my life.' he commended her actions as he cuddled her.

'Thank him for saving us both', she referred to the driver.

'Thanks boss', he voiced it louder to the driver.

'It's a pleasure', the driver responded. *'You're not the first one. It's not safe to be around late into the night. Where are we heading to?'*

'The uni please' Timbo answered in relief.

'Oh, so you are new to the place. Be careful the next time'.

The taxi dropped them off in front of Janet's building. Despite struggling their rough night, neither wanted to leave where they were dropped off. They just wanted to be with each other to compensate for the lost plan. But they could not; they had to part to avoid unwanted consequences. The security officer was prying from the corner. Thus, they eventually parted; she stood and waved from her door while he slowly disappeared into the darkness waving like a parent leaving his daughter at the 'Daycare Centre' for the first time.

That was uni.

Ducking the duck

Studies were getting a bit tough. The workload was getting heavier. Timbo had to dig his shoes in further if he had to get through. When the assessment came through before the study week, he noted that his maths average was far below the expectation. The only way to get through was to pass the exam in the 90 - 100% band. Thus he refrained from joining his mates for any social events the weeks before the exam and put in 150% effort in his studies.

Timbo would not even open his door to anyone knocking after dinner so he could concentrate. At dinner his mates were questioning his wellbeing. *'Are you ok? We haven't seen much of you these days, what happened?'*, queried Chrisko his senior mate.

'Yeah man, who's the unlucky bird in the cage now?', joked the other one. *'Maybe we should have a cuppa in his room tonight'*, joined the others. They were all making joking comments but Timbo only absorbed and shared in the fun but did not reveal the cause of his sudden anti-socialisation when first questioned. He just kept them wondering and hoped no one would visit him during the nights to disturb his study rhythm.

However, he was about to lie down the following night to do some reading in bed when he heard someone calling from the door after knocking. It was Chrisko's voice. He had to open the door; he was Timbo's mentor when first arrived at uni.

'Why the hell are you coming at this time of the night', Timbo jokingly asked as he opened the door to him.

'*Oh come on. You can't spend all your life studying. Where's the kettle?*' he asked. Timbo opened the cupboard and Chrisko took and filled it up. Timbo steered away from his desk and faced Chrisko making coffee for them. '*I thought you've got someone here that kept you from joining us these days*', joked Chrisko.

'*Do you think I'd open the door if there was?*', countered Timbo while laughing over coffee. '*I'd say you're very sneaky coming at this time of the night when everyone is about to hit the bed*', added Timbo.

'*Well why do you think I would come at this time of night?*', Chrisko commented. '*You can only do it to your best friend*', he justified.

'*And what can your best friend do?*', questioned Timbo humorously.

'*A HA! you've got me there*', agreed Chrisko. '*That's exactly why I'm here. I need your help. I've been to our other mates and you are my last resort*'. With a change of tone, he slowly said, '*My mum is seriously ill at home and I want to visit her but I do not have enough money for my fare. Can you can spare any to supplement it? I'll pay you back upon returning*'.

'*But who said I have any spare money?*', teased Timbo

They continued their jokes over their coffee while Timbo pulled out his bank book from his draw. He opened it in front of Chrisko and said, '*Look, that's all I have in my savings, seventy bucks, ($70), and that's all I can offer if it does make a difference*', he offered.

'*That's more than enough mate*', acknowledged Chrisko.

'*In that case we may as well skip our first lectures tomorrow and be the first customers in the bank to withdraw all of it and pay your fare for the first available flight*', Timbo suggested.

Chrisko was a bit emotional at Timbo's receptiveness before he said, '*Man you are a legend. Thank you so much for your understanding attitude*', he commended Timbo.

'*Oh don't say that; we all have parents. Someday I will need your help too but I'm sorry that's all I can offer*', Timbo sympathetically responded.

'*It's very much appreciated. Thanks a lot*', returned Chrisko.

'*How long are you going for?*', asked Timbo.

'*For a week at the most. But it depends on her condition*', answered Chrisko.

'*I hope she gets better*'.

'*I hope so too. I want to be back before the exam week. I'm a bit behind my studies*'.

'*Me too, that's why I'm cutting out on our get together these days. I don't want to be on the plane empty-handed like a batsman leaving the pitch with a duck. I love my parents too*', declared Timbo. It was the first time he revealed the cause of refraining from socialisation when queried by his mates.

'*Well, thanks for the coffee and most importantly your sympathetic response. Sorry for disturbing your studies. I better leave you to your studies. I'll see you tomorrow*', Chrisko concluded the night.

'*Don't worry; we'll all be in trouble one day or another. I hope things turn out well for you. I'll see you first thing tomorrow*'.

When Chrisko returned the following week, he did not forget his promise to repay Timbo. It was the same day and at the same time of that week that he knocked again on Timbo's door, '*The shop is closed*', Timbo responded as the knock got louder. '*There's no more sugar*', he called as he walked to open the door.

It was Chrisko again, '*That was fast. When did you come back*', he inquired.

'*This morning*', replied Chrisko

'*How's your mum?*'

'*That's why I'm back sooner. She's getting better thanks*', Chrisko answered in relief.

'*That's very good news*', sympathized Timbo as he boiled the kettle for their cuppa.

After their cups of tea, Chrisko handed Timbo the envelope, '*Here*'.

'*What's that?*' Timbo questioned.

52

'I was very honored with your help; without which I would't have made it home to see my mum'.

'Do you think I will take it?' asked Timbo. *'No way. Don't be stupid. If I take it back, I will not let you in again the next time. I'm just glad I've been able to help you. We are all students and we are all trying to help each other one way or another. Keep it and pay me back when we qualify and working fulltime at home',* he lectured Chrisko as he pushed the envelope back to Chrisko.

'Are you sure?', reaffirmed Chrisko asked.

'I'm positive my friend', Timbo confirmed.

Chrisko was astounded at Timbo's gesture. He got up and hugged Timbo, *'I don't know what to say about your thoughtfulness. You are more than a friend'.*

'Yeah, your tea boy too', Timbo cracked a joke to relieve Chrisko's emotions before they finally called it a night.

Choice Privilege

When Timbo went home for the long vacation, he scored a place in the only main public hospital laboratory to get some hospital experience. He liked it too, not only for experience but also for some pocket money for the holiday.

It was a good time, Timbo reflected. He did not do much solid work but shown various aspects of the workload faced by employees each day. On the second Friday since starting, the boss of the Laboratory came over to him and said, *'The Medical Director has asked for you to see him this afternoon at 2pm'.*

'Thanks', Timbo answered. *'Will you have any idea of what that could be about?',* he asked.

'Sorry, but I don't know', the boss responded. Timbo did not have any lunch but was worried over the upcoming confrontation with the Medical Director. He was speculating that he probably did not do well in his exams.

At 2.00 o'clock, he was already sweating outside the director's office. As soon as he saw the director coming, he smartly got up and let him through as if he was going to salute the director. The director smiled and turned to shake Timbo's hand.

'*Come in*', he invited Timbo as he opened the office for him. '*Take a seat*', he offered. '*How are you?*', he asked Timbo diplomatically.

'*I'm ok thanks*', Timbo replied in a more controlled tone.

'*How are enjoying your holiday?*', the director continued as he tried to ease Timbo's nervousness.

'*It's very rewarding. The staff members are very friendly*', he responded passionately.

'*That's good to hear. How about your studies?*', the director pressed on.

With a bit of worry, Timbo said, '*It was tough at times but I tried my best*'.

'*Good. That's why I called to see you. I'm very happy with your results. There are two specialist fields of studies currently on offer, thanks to the WHO's sponsorship, the Optometry and Radiography. Before we advertise I thought I would give you the priority based on your results if you are interested*', declared the director.

Timbo's facial expression was enough to reveal his confusion to the director. Before he responded, the director continued, '*Optometry will be taken in the US while Radiography will be done at your current institute for three years*'.

Timbo knew nothing about both these fields. Thus, he was not scared to ask the director, '*Sorry sir, but I don't know anything about these two fields. Can you please elaborate a bit?*'.

'*Sure, Optometry is the study of eyes for defects or abnormalities and management of eye diseases. Radiography is the study of radiation to provide images and data for the diagnosis and treatment of patients*', the director explained.

Timbo was off guard; he was not expecting this sort of scenario. Both fields sounded novel enough to make any quick decision on but he had to give the director an answer before leaving the ofice. He thought of taking Optometry but it would mean cutting off his mates. Also, it would be too far from his parents should anything untoward happen. Thus, he told the director, *'I'll take Radiography sir if that's ok with you'*.

'Congratulations, that's very good. I'll get things organised for you then and will call you again if I need anything', the director stated.

'Thank you sir', Timbo acknowledged.

'Don't thank me son. I'm only here to make sure the help from our kind sponsors, especially the World Health Organisation, is put into proper use for the future of our country. We thank them dearly for their kind donations. Enjoy the rest of your holiday', the director professed while shaking Timbo's hand on his way out.

Timbo was not quite sure of his choice just made. On one hand he regretted it because he had never been to the US and this would have been a golden opportunity for him to go. On the other hand, it would be handy for home visits. But he had already made his decision; he had to live with it.

The Last Plane Ride

After Timbo received his first pay, he went back to his village to visit his family especially his father who was reportedly sick. His parents and the rest of his siblings were very elated to see him again since leaving for the first time. Nothing seemed to change much to him excepting that his father looked pale and frail.

Timbo's arrival injected some new energy into him. It made him revert to his usual dominating self that distinguished him from the rest of oldies back home; a character that often created tension between him and Timbo's mother. She was very reserved and conservative while he was very jovial and impetuous.

When Timbo was ready to return to work, he had already made a plan to take his parents with him. But his wage could only pay for him and one other person in the inter-island flight. He talked it over with his parents and siblings and his mother agreed to come in the ferry with one of the siblings while Timbo and his father took the flight.

The airfield was a fifteen minute drive from home. It was an unsealed one. When the plane arrived, it had to fly over the whole runway first in a very low altitude to chase off any strayed animal before it landed. Moreover, the southern end of the runway crossed path with the main coastal highway. Before landing or take-off, vehicles had to be stopped to let the plane through. The only maintenance accorded by the villagers nearby was grass cutting and helped chasing animals away before landing and take-off.

This was a simple basic airstrip with no control tower or fire engine; it was suitable mainly for emergency airlifts like those in war zone. However, it was still functional as a commercial civilian service from the locals' point of view. Thus, it continued to supply the service without much hassle or even a disaster.

When Timbo entered the plane, he wanted to sit with his father but was given the last single seat at the back while his dad was given the one in the front. Timbo felt like sitting on the floor with his knees almost to his chin. He looked over to check on his dad, his seat was a bit high and cushioned. His only concern then was his inability to help his dad should anything happen to the flight. He was also concerned that he might not fulfil his promise to his mother and other siblings and he would bear the blame for taking him away from the comfort of their home even though he needed medical attention.

When the plane taxied for take-off, he could feel every minor bump. He was not at all surprised considering the condition of the airstrip but was very impressed at how gutsy the pilot was in braving the field. The sea was approaching faster and the plane was still taxiing. He was stretching up to see if they would ever take off when the plane slowly raised its nose before reaching the sea. He finally breathed a relieving sigh. He was scared they could have ended in an unwanted swim if the plane failed to take off.

It was the first time Timbo paid for his father's flight from his first pay. It was also Timbo's first and last plane ride together with his father from this airstrip before returning to resume studies. Without Timbo's preconceived knowledge, this was also their last plane ride together before life took its turn on his father.

The Sticky Peak

While Timbo was training in the base hospital, he was exposed to some of the staff members' talk on the advanced level of the same course in Australia. It inspired him but did not know who to turn to for further information. He gathered that it would be a facilitating door to enter if he could get entrance into it. But it would be just a matter of keeping his ears opened for any staff member that could give more information on it.

When he returned from holiday he was introduced to Chen, a former employee of the department returning from Australia for a home visit. He gained employment in Australia after graduating from the advanced course Timbo was interested in. Chen took up a temporary job in the department again to catch up with his former colleagues. On the other hand, the boss reckoned it best of a chance to share his Aussie skill with the locals.

Chen was very open with everyone. Timbo thought he would be the best source of information on the advanced course he heard of.

One of Timbo's classmates had a chance to talk with Chen and asked how he got into the advanced radiography course in Australia. Chen did not hesitate to answer and explained in great detail the steps he took to get there. Timbo was working nearby; he overheard the conversation and listened in out of interest.

As soon as Chen quoted the school's address to Timbo's classmate, Timbo wasted no time and scribbled it down his notebook. He too was interested in the course even though he was only halfway through the current one.

Once he got back to his room he quickly drafted a letter to the school Chen mentioned.

Timbo regarded it to be too good of a chance to see Australia, and another opportunity to advance his career. After dinner, he did not stay around to chat with his friends as usual but worked on his application letter to be sent the following morning. He thought his sponsor would not mind using his pocket money to pay for this course if accepted. It was the same field in a more advanced level. When he sent it, it was only addressed to the principal of the school but was not sure if that was the right channel.

After a month of waiting, he received a letter from the school students' liaison officer acknowledging his letter with a request to submit his exam results in the current institute for further consideration. Timbo was more than relieved and excited that his letter had finally got through.

He set about collecting and collating all the documents required and sent them to the liaison officer. Though he was progressing well with his current course, it did not mean he would be guaranteed acceptance to the new one.

He still had to finish the current course in high stead if his ambition was to keep advancing. Moreover, this was the basis of his sponsorship; any underperformance in the current one would sever his sponsorship and hence hinder his ambition for future advancement.

The Fall of the Pillar

One Saturday after breakfast when Timbo was on his desk trying to study, he heard someone knocking on his door. '*Oh no, not now. Please go away I want to study*', he pleaded mentally thinking it could be his mates trying to come in for a weekend yarn. He sat still very quietly making the intruder think there was no one in the room. But then he heard his friend calling the intruder, '*He's probably stepped out for something. He could not be far away*'.

From then he concluded it could not be one of his mates. He quickly jumped to the door and opened to check. To his surprise, he saw a young man with a helmet and in a neat bikie's dress. When he turned around, he was the postman. He turned to Timbo and asked, '*Hi! Are you Timbo?*'.

'*Yes, what can I do?*', Timbo answered with anxiety.

'*This is for you*', the postman produced the envelope and left.

'*Thanks*', Timbo acknowledged the service and disappeared into his room again.

Upon opening the envelope, it was a telegram from his government, reading:

'*Dear Timbo,*

Your father is seriously ill. We have organised for you to take the first flight back home. Please contact the local airline for the time of the flight.

With kind regards.

Tjudei Thomas (government secretary)'.

Timbo kept staring at the telegram and tried to come to terms with the unlikely consequences. The government would only do such move in serious cases. It was obvious to Timbo his father's condition was terminal for the government not only to inform him but also organise his flight home. Thus he had to organise himself fast and prepare for the worse.

Things were in frenzy all of a sudden. The incentive to study disappeared abruptly. He was then quick to realise how his mate felt when he came over for financial help to visit his mother sometime in the past. It was his turn then. His friend had already qualified and back at home; but Timbo was on his own here. He had no one to lean on right now, not financially but for moral support. He had to think and think hard. Instead of studying any further, he began packing.

When one of his mates knocked later on, Timbo was sweating furiously not only from packing but also from stress over any unfavorable consequences of his call.

'Are you alright? Why did the postman come?' Banjo asked.

'My dad's sick. It must be serious for our government to send a telegram. That's why I'm packing now', Timbo answered in a depressed tone.

'I'm sorry', Banjo sympathized. *'But don't be depressed. You've done him a very good favour by winning a scholarship to be here. Not all families have it. He must be very proud of you'*, encouraged Banjo.

'Thanks bro. But I still want him to be there when I finish so he can see the end result of his dream' Timbo poured out his discomfort.

'That's your part to play to honour him by finishing the course, isn't it?', Banjo tried keeping the light in Timbo's tunnel.

'Thanks again. You are a real friend, you've got a point. I'll remember that', acknowledged Timbo.

'Let's go for a cuppa and then I'll help you packing when we return', Banjo added. Timbo stood for a second before finally giving in.

'Ok', as he opened the door for him.

Banjo knew he had to distract Timbo from the after effect of the telegram. Thus, he forced himself to create jokes and made-up stories to lighten the mood and make their tea tasty. They had a nursing sister working in the department they were based in. Banjo used her as a distraction, *'Remember sister Nanja'*, he asked Timbo.

'Yeah, what about her?', enquired Timbo.

'She got her driving licence last weekend. When she left on Monday, she said she did not want anyone to distract her when driving. But when she left, Theo took us to the corner where sister would drive through to await her. As soon as she came around we all cheered and waved to her from both sides of the road and she did not know who to look at', Banjo laughed as he was trying to finish.

'And then?' Timbo asked eagerly.

'And when she came the following morning, she was very upset and she blew all of us off'.

'And?' Timbo plodded as they laughed their way to the cafeteria.

'No one cared. They made fun of her even more'.

'Did the boss say anything?' Timbo was interested.

'He was just laughing when he got the full story', concluded Banjo as they shared the fun of the story.

Before they returned their cups, Sherri, their classmate, called up from the Table Tennis room, *'Hey, its Tag team now if you want to join'*.

'Well, why not. Is it our turn now?', asked Banjo.

'If you want', she enticed them.

Timbo was a bit hesitant but Banjo pushed him in the room to distract him from depression. *'There's plenty of time. We'll have one game if we can't beat these guys'*, he prompted Timbo as they entered the room.

It was not just one game.

Once Banjo and Timbo started, they kept teasing the winning team and managed to upset them until the other team lost. On a winning streak, Timbo and Banjo were on the table till lunchtime.

By then Timbo appeared to be over his gloominess, thanks to Banjo's friendship. Lunch was even tastier than it would have been earlier. They even hung around the cafeteria longer with the other students after lunch as if nothing had happened. It was only after all the students had left that they finally returned to Timbo's room to complete packing.

On Monday Timbo received a call from the X-ray department where he was based for training, *'Good morning, this is Timbo'*, he answered.

'Hi Timbo, this is Ken. How are you?' Timbo's heart started to thumb louder; this was the department's director calling. He never called Timbo before but it was obvious something's happened.

'I'm ok sir,' Timbo forced his voice through.

'I'm sorry to hear about your father. I have given consent to your government's request to release you so you can attend his funeral. The staff members are sending their sympathies for you and wish you a safe trip', he added.

'Thank you sir', Timbo tried to mutter while tears came pouring down his cheeks. His boss said something before he hung up but his vision and hearing were all blurry.

Timbo collapsed onto his bed and could not hold his emotions in anymore. Things started to get fuzzy from then on. *'The pillar of my study is now gone, what's the point of continuing?'* he cried and asked himself while trying to come to terms with the news.

It was not long before he was called to take another phone call. This time it was the airline telling him a taxi had been arranged for him in an hour's time to take him to the airport. A ticket would be awaiting him there; all he had to do was to present his passport upon arrival at the counter.

Timbo did not care about the state of his room then. He was just throwing anything into his suitcase to be ready before the taxi arrived. When he got at the airport, he was the last one on the plane. He was sweating and unsettled after the many hiccups he had to attend to before catching the taxi. But he was grateful he had made it on the plane.

Everyone seemed to be all in tune with his mood until the flight was halfway when the atmosphere changed. He realised he was travelling with his country's sports team returning from the South Pacific Games, the mini version of the Olympic. They were in high spirit after winning medals from the games. Thus, they were celebrating their successes in the plane as if they were in a pub. The effect of alcohol had made them singing and enjoying their trip; a behavior that dearly exacerbated his grief.

When the captain popped out of the cockpit for a brief moment, he was shocked to see them out of control. He did not say a thing but disappeared into the cockpit again. Before long, the plane sounded as if it was ascending and the seatbelt warning started to blink. It started to shake a bit too and the captain's voice came through warning passengers of few bumps on the way.

As warned, they weren't just bumps but it was turbulent enough to get hold of something before thrown off their seats. It was long enough to break the party. By the time it calmed down, the joy riders had vanished into their seats surrendering their drinks for their safety.

When the captain appeared again, they all looked sober again as if there was no party before. He gave a scoffing smile as if to say, *'That's the only way to fix you guys if you don't know how to behave'*.

Sitting across the aisle was the team manager. His tummy almost touched the seat in front of him. Thus when the air hostess came along with the tray of lollies for the passengers to clear their blocked ears during the flight ascending and descending, he just swiped them all onto his big tummy without considering other passengers. Timbo did not care. All he wanted was to get home sooner rather than later. He could not stand facing the team's behavior during these dark hours.

Upon landing, he rushed out to be away from them all and took a taxi to the wharf fifteen minutes away from the airport. Once on the ferry home, he recalled vividly the incidences that happened on his first trip with his dad to the capital and his new school. He even recalled their last trip together he paid in the small plane before returning to uni. He was then alone upon returning home. It was a very nostalgic flashback.

Tears could not be shed. Timbo tried valiantly to hold the tears back. He was, nonetheless, grateful he had at least done a favour for his father as a token of gratitude for all the hard work he had done in getting him and his siblings to where they are now.

'*What now? Shall I return to study or shall I better stay put and look after my mum now that dad's gone?*' he kept asking himself while trying to absorb the pain of losing his father. He thought he would wait his mother's word on whether or not to return to study when things started settling down.

After the funeral, he finally had a chance to chat with his mum privately. Timbo confided his worries and concerns about continuing his studies. His mother listened intently and described his father's last days with them. '*Your father's word for you when I asked him, was not to interfere with your studies but to send you his love*'. They both were in tears but Timbo was more relieved then that his uncertainty had finally cleared.

'*What about you? What do you think? Shall I return to continue my studies now that Dad is not here?*', he asked.

'*Of course, yes*', his mother affirmed. '*Your dad sacrificed everything, even his life, for your sake. I will be even more comforted if you make it through than to stay half done. We can only be thankful to your sponsors for their kind donations. Without them your father's dream for you would not be achieved. That's why you should never back down but continue*', she asserted.

Timbo's benefit of doubt was then absolved. He had to return, not only to provide comfort to his mother but also as a dedication to his father's memory. It was also an acknowledgement of his sponsor's kindness.

On the day of his return, the weather was not looking good. It was raining very heavily. Timbo remembered the rough weather he experienced on his previous trip and was not looking forward to this one.

It was not long after take-off when, the warning sign for seatbelts came up on the screen. The captain's voice followed warning all passengers of the turbulent weather ahead.

Timbo could see lightning and felt the thumbing of the thunder. The plane started to be thrown up and down. He was in deep concern if he had done anything wrong for all these unfortunate things to happen. He was still suffering from his father's loss, and now this sort of weather offered no consolation. He was not sure if they would ever land.

Timbo slowly pushed up the window blind to peek outside, but it was only the fierce darkness lightened by threatening lightning. He pulled it down again and held tight on to his seat. The flight attendants were nowhere to be seen while everyone was super quiet. The whole flight was unquestionably very frightening.

All of a sudden an announcement came through, *'Is there a Doctor or medical personnel in the flight? Please reveal yourself to the stewards; your help is greatly needed'.*

'Someone has fallen sick', Timbo's neighbour finally opened up to him.

'I'm not surprised. The weather is horrible', Timbo tried to respond while holding hard on his seat's arms.

Soon after the announcement, the air hostess rushed across the aisle with the small portable oxygen bottle. A middle aged man, looking like a medical personnel if not a Doctor, followed her. He was holding onto the seat's head rests as he tried to defy the unsteadiness of the plane to reach the patient.

'It doesn't look good', Timbo's neighbour tried to keep the dialogue.

'No, it doesn't. I hope things get better', Timbo offered a sympathetic response.

It was not long before they saw the air hostess and the man return. The problem was probably fixed, Timbo thought.

Another announcement followed, *'Many thanks for the kind assistance and immediate response. Everything seems to be ok now. But please keep your seat belts on until cleared by the captain. Thanks again'.*

When the stewardesses finally pushed their trolleys for refreshments no one seemed interested. It looked like all they yearned for then was the plane to land sooner and safely.

Timbo finally breathed a great relieving sigh when he heard the plane's wheels roared thru the tarmac. A loud round of applause swept through the plane as it taxied to the terminal. It was the most frightening flight he had ever taken.

'That was scary', said his neighbor.

'Very scary', agreed Timbo. *'Thank God we made it. I thought we'd be blown away somewhere up there',* he added jokingly as they made their way to the terminal.

The Double Dip

Upon returning to uni, Timbo's morale was very low for a while. It was not until after he received a letter from the Royal Melbourne Institute of Technology informing him of his acceptance to the Australian advanced course that his attitude changed. His mates observed Timbo's changes and were happy too.

'Hey what happened?' asked his mate Bao. *'Its good you are cheering up now'.*

Timbo did not rush to say anything but just returned their inquiries with a smile that baffled them.

'Well, come on, aren't you going to tell us your secret?' joined Banjo.

Timbo remembered their efforts in trying to cheer him up before he went to his father's funeral. He thought this would be the good time to acknowledge their sympathy by sharing his news.

'Yeah, I have some good news', he announced.

'What is it?' prompted Bao.

'I have been accepted for the advanced course in Australia starting next year', he revealed.

'A what? A course in Australia? Wow, congrats my friend', commended Banjo.

'Yeah mate, that's very good news', added Bao.

'So how are you going to do that with your current course?' asked Bao.

'They are happy with my results from here and they've exempted me from doing first year. So, while I'll be doing my final year here, I'll be doing the second year of theirs by correspondence', Timbo explained.

'That sounds good but it could be a bit overburden to you by the sound of things', warned Bao.

'He should be alright', supported Banjo. *'My only concern is the funding. Are you paying it yourself?'*, queried Banjo.

'Yeah, I'll try and save as much as I can of my pocket money from now on to pay for it. I don't think my sponsor will mind. They should be happy I'm not wasting it but using it for the advanced level of the same course'.

'That's right. You're killing two pigeons with one arrow. Our government will be happy too', added Bao.

'Well, good on you mate. What a time to receive it', cheered Banjo.

'Yeah man. Your dad must have left his blessing for you', joked Bao.

'Can be', approved Timbo. He looked up the sky and called, 'Thanks Dad'.

Displaced Discrimination

At the end of his final year, Timbo did not rush going home because he wanted to celebrate the end of his studies. His classmates were doing the same.

The end of year results was always posted on the school's notice board. Timbo did not bother looking soon after the results were posted. He was confident of his efforts and was sure that he sailed through without a hitch.

It was only after dinner that he learnt his fate. One of his school mates came around for their usual post dinner talk and offered a casual comment,

'I'm sorry mate', he consoled Timbo.

'For what?', Timbo responded in shock.

'Oh, didn't you see the results?'

'You're kidding. This can't be true. How can I miss this easy exam when I got through my Aussie one which is a lot tougher?', retorted Timbo. He abruptly got up and rushed to the board which was a few meters away from the dining hall.

To his surprise, not one of his classmates passed. It was obvious that something was not right that failed them all. His body was shaking. 'How can they do this to me and my mates', he tried to comprehend it. He was trying to recall any equivocal incidence he and his classmates did to annoy their tutors in the training department; that could be the only cause for all of them to get such results.

On the following morning he gathered his classmates and tried to resolve the problem before the graduation. They all agreed to approach the Uni student's representative to present their case to have a bit more weighting. After working on the letter of protest outlining their case, Timbo and his friends met up with the Uni students' representative and went through all the points they raised to address the issue.

Timbo and his friends were then referred to the Dean to present their case. From there, they found out that it was the training department that failed them. Thus, they made an appointment with the department director to sort out why they had all failed the course.

'Well, there's nothing much I can do', replied the department director. 'When you fail, you fail', he concluded regardless of the students' representative's effort to verify the points in the letter. It was obvious they were fighting a losing battle. The director offered no sympathy at all but stood by his subordinates' decision.

When they came out of the conference room, they were all furious at the departmental director's attitude.

'I'm sorry but we could not help you', apologised the students' representative. 'You will eventually find out the cause of this unfairness someday, but for your sake, you have to bear with it and come back next year to finish this off', encouraged the student rep.

'Are we going through it again for another full year', asked Timbo.

'No, usually the supplementary exam takes place after three months', the student representative replied. 'Is there anything else I can help you?'.

'I don't think so but many thanks for your kind assistance', they all thanked him before he left.

All of a sudden, they were all at a loss. They could not believe such a thing could happen after going through the previous years of the course without a struggle. They finally ended up consoling each other and pledged to return the following year to re-sit their final exams.

Despite Timbo's frustration over his final exams he was relieved with his examination results from his Australian one; it was like passing a driving test on a busy street but failed in a quiet one.

The truth of their failures was only revealed to him when he returned to complete the course the following three months. Timbo found out later from one of the staff members that one of Timbo's classmates had a clash with the Head Tutor before the exams. Thus, the whole class had to bear the consequences to avoid discriminatory accusations.

4th door: The Aussie Call

The Trip Misadventure

When Timbo returned home after completing the first course, he had the clinical component of the Australian course to complete. Thus, he was offered another scholarship to pursue in the RMIT University, Australia. Timbo was used to travelling during his years of overseas studies. He never had any problem wearing shoes. But this trip was different. He started feeling his shoes tightness at the start of the flight but he did not give it much thought. He assumed it would go away after a while. However, as the plane climbed higher and higher, the pain got worse and worse until he could not stand it anymore.

To relieve the pressure, Timbo removed his shoes – a move he regretted later.

When he went to the bathroom in socks only, he was shocked to feel something cold on his feet. His socks had soaked up something on the floor. He was very appalled. He felt sick with the sudden soddening of his socks as if someone had underestimated his distance and ended up in wetting the toilet floor.

Without hesitation, he quickly withdrew himself from the toilet and plodded back to his seat. Unsure of what to do, he slowly slid his socks away from his feet without touching them and hoped they'd be dry by the time the plane landed. He tried to make himself comfortable and hoped no smell would spring up from the wet socks to annoy his neighbouring passenger or be suspected of doing something childish.

Luckily, the plane landed before any unpleasant smell could be detected. The socks were half dry but he had to put them on again to continue the trip.

Timbo discovered that there was a quite a distance to walk from the plane to the next gate. But he was then plagued with wet socks and tight shoes. Thus, as soon as he saw a toilet sign, he ducked for it without a second look whether it's for ladies or men.

'*Excuse me, excuse me*', someone called relentlessly from outside.

Timbo did not take heed of the call but rushed in, took the first bench he got to and started taking his shoes off. Groaning in deep agony, he tried to massage them vigorously to relieve the pain. As soon as the pain was bearable, he cautiously put the shoes on again, tied the laces up very loosely and came out again.

To his surprise he was met by the cleaner and the security officer at the door. '*Did you know what you were doing?*', blasted the security officer.

'*No*', Timbo answered innocently. Looking lost and confused, he wondered, '*What's wrong?*'.

'*Whats wrong?*', repeated the security officer in disbelief,

'*Can't you see the big sign saying "LADIES"?*', he continued in a very imposing voice.

'*Oh! I'm sorry. My feet were so painful that I only wanted somewhere to take my shoes off without having a proper look first*', Timbo apologized.

'*Can I have a look at your passport?*', the officer demanded.

While Timbo was reaching for his passport, the officer asked again, '*Where are you off to?*'.

'*Australia sir*', replied Timbo in a remorseful voice while handling over his passport. He could not hide his fear through the sweat running all of a sudden like a busted tap. The officer could see it.

After skimming through the passport, *'Well, I will let you off this time. But you better watch where you're going the next time because you'll end up in biiig big trouble',* he warned.

Timbo thanked him again.

When glancing over to the cleaner, she was not impressed. She just gave a scoffing grin that aggravated Timbo's embarrassment. He quickly turned away from them and headed for his gate.

'Don't forget this', the security officer called. When he turned, it was his passport. He was in total panic. *'Thanks again sir,'* was his final words and tried to disappear from this site in no seconds.

Walking away, Timbo could not believe such a thing could happen. He was heading for higher education and yet he could not read basic signs on his way. Despite the pain recurring again with his feet, he sped off to his gate in no time.

While still reeling from his aching feet in the waiting area, he overheard someone whispering loudly, *'Nice Bola'.* Looking up to see where the voice came from, there was a young local lady watching him from the row facing him. She gave a smile. He returned a complimentary grin. He knew the words she whispered meant 'nice person'. This time it did not mean much to him because of his pain.

He forced a smile back. He was still trying to get over the previous debacle. His feet weren't any help. He just wanted to be in a secluded space where he could remove his shoes and give his feet a good massage. Before he could do it, he saw the same security officer again going up to the reception at his waiting area.

The next thing he heard was an announcement, *'Calling Mr Timbo Aristo, please report to the counter if you are in the waiting area'.*

Embarrassed and in agony, he braved himself to the front desk in no time to avoid being called again. The security officer turned around and said, *'Hello sir, I'm sorry to call you again but I have to make an incidence report on what happened. Do you mind?'.*

'No' mumbled Timbo. He knew he had no choice.

'*Come with me please*', ordered the security officer.

'*Oh! No, this is turning into a nightmare*', pondered Timbo. While worried of missing his flight, he could also be sent home from here.

The officer opened the door and to his surprise, there was another lady officer sitting at the desk and of course the cleaner he confronted earlier.

'*Hello Sir*', greeted the lady officer. '*I'm Cathy, I'm the officer in charge of ladies security and welfare in the airport*', she introduced herself. She turned to the cleaner and continued, '*This is Fifi who saw you entering the facility without taking heed of her call. Do you recognise her?*

'*Yes, madam*', Timbo tried to force his voice in reply.

'*Did you hear her call?*', she queried.

'*Yes madam*',

'*Why didn't you respond?*'

'*I was not aware she was calling me*'.

'*Did you see the sign saying* 'LADIES'*?*'

'*No madam*'.

'*Can you read?*'.

'*Yes Madam*'.

'*How come you did not see the big sign?*'.

Before Timbo answered again, '*What do you do?*', she kept going.

'*I'm a radiographer?*'

'*A radio what?*'.

'*A radiographer*'

'*What's that?*' she double checked with the male officer, '*Do you know that?*'. The male officer just shrugged his shoulders in limbo but said nothing.

'*Taking images of patients using X-rays*', answered Timbo in a bit of a relief that he knew something they did not.

'*Where are you heading to?*' she pressed on.

'*Australia*',

'*Why?*

'*For further studies*'.

'**For further studies?**' she repeated slowly and in an elevated tone. '*You are going for further studies and yet you could not read the big* 'LADIES' *sign?*. She looked straight at Timbo. She was not impressed. Timbo felt his tummy rumbling in protest but could not express it.

'*Do you smoke?*', she kept bombarding Timbo.

'*No madam.*'

'*Drink?*'

'*No madam.*'

'*Are you married?*'

'*No madam.*'

'*So there you are*', she looked at the male officer as if she had hit the jackpot in Timbo's cause of action. The male officer just returned a nodding gesture but did not say a word.

'*Typical adventurous youngsters trying to beat the system*', she sighed.

'*Look, your action doesn't agree with your declaration. That's why we have to search you now. Do you understand me?*', she explained Timbo.

'*Yes madam*', he answered bravely. He could feel a wave of numbness crawling like a spider throughout his body. He was on his own. He had no one but himself to blame.

He was shown another door behind the lady officer. He thought it would only be the male security officer, but to his surprise, the female officer was right behind him.

'*Alright, take everything off*', ordered the male officer.

Before he dropped them away the lady officer picked them up and checked all pockets and clothing creases for anything that might drop off.

Timbo was standing naked with only the undie on when he was ordered, *'Your undie off as well, thank you'.*

He looked at the female officer as if begging for leniency but there was no sympathy, *'Come on, undie off',* she reinforced the order.

Timbo timorously removed his undie and stood fully naked for the first time in front of anyone. He felt as if his whole life was gone. He was like another animal paraded in an auction for someone to care for. But there were only two bidders present; they were from the same stake though, the law. And the verdict was, *'Get dressed again',* ordered the male security officer. The female one had vanished into the office again.

Back in the consulting room, the lady officer declared, *'We are satisfied with everything. Do you have any questions?'*

'No madam', replied Timbo in relief let alone the embarrassment.

'Ok sign here. This certifies that you understood the procedure we've been through and that you consented to its execution. Agreed?', she reconfirmed while he was given the form to sign.

'Yes madam', Timbo responded softly while signing the form.

'You can go now. Have a safe trip', embarked the lady officer.

While shown the door, the officer called in an enlightening tone, *'Don't forget to buy cleaner undies the next time',* she joked. Timbo grinned back but did not want to know them. He could not believe the embarrassment he had been through then, all because of his agony.

The next thing he heard over the speaker was the announcement, *'Final Call for Mr Timbo Aristo, please go straight to Gate 22 for your flight check in'.*

Timbo weaved speedily amongst the crowd to get to the gate. He knew it would be more embarrassing to be deported home when missing the flight than the incidence he just had. When he made it to the gate, the lady at the desk stopped him, *'I'm sorry, but the gate is closed'.*

'But I've just been called to come to the gate', countered Timbo.

'I know, but you should have been here at least an hour before boarding', the attendant stood her ground.

'*I was here then but I was called away by the security officer*', countered Timbo. He knew that if he backed down he would either be deported home or pay extra for another flight to continue and even pay a hotel to await the next flight. But he was under sponsorship; his trip itinerary had been planned so that his arrival at his destination coincided with the one awaiting him. If he missed the flight he would have no way of communication with whoever was waiting.

Luckily the officer that called him to the desk remembered it and called out, '*Yes, he's right. The security officer asked me to call him. Why don't you call the supervising attendant if they can take him?*' she pleaded her colleague.

The refusing officer gave him a gloomy look but he was not deterred. He remained hopeful he would be given entry.

After turning her back and making a phone call, she turned around with a sudden change of face and smiled, '*You're lucky. They are happy to spare a minute for you. But remember to be early the next time. Have a safe trip*', she added.

Joyously, Timbo could not stop saying, '*Thank you, thank you*', while dancing his way to the plane. He had finally made it to Australia.

The Thrill of Arriving Sydney Airport

Timbo was overwhelmed with the size of the airport he had arrived at. He was even more dumfounded with the glittering welcome from the many shops lining their way out like different platoons giving a guard of honour to a royal arrival. While keeping his cool and trying to absorb all the new sights, he was also trying to keep up with other passengers of his flight so that he would not repeat the previous misadventure.

Upon arrival at the intersection with one arrow pointing to '**LUGGAGE PICK UP**' sign and another pointing to '**TRANSIT**', he slowed down to a stop and started wondering whether to follow the former for his luggage, or the latter assuming his luggage would turn up at the final destination. It was not long before he heard a helpful voice, '*Are you alright sir?*', she was one of the passengers.

'*No, I'm heading to Melbourne; this is my first time in Australia and I'm at a loss of which arrow to follow*', he tried to explain.

'*Don't worry, follow me*', she enlightened.

'*Thanks.*'

'*My pleasure*', she returned and tried to slow down for him so they could walk together but Timbo was also slowing down so she could lead the way.

'*We'll be taking a bus to the Domestic Terminal to catch the next flight*', she tried to open a conversation with Timbo.

'*I see. Do you have to pay for a ticket?*', he responded in wonder.

'*No. Your flight ticket is your bus ticket and buses are allocated flight numbers for their trips*'. she confirmed.

'*What about my luggage?*', he asked.

'*They are transferred directly to the next flight and be picked up at final destination*', she assured Timbo.

'*Really?*' he followed it up with excitement.

'*Yep*'.

'*That's nice of them*', he sighed.

'*It's the way the system runs*', she explained.

Timbo's eyes could not stop marvelling at the glitter of the airport as they exited to the 'Bus Pick Up' spot. He was just like another sheep following his new found guide.

Upon arrival at the domestic terminal, he followed her to the check-in desk. But when he reached for his wallet he could not find it. He felt both back pockets of his trousers and he could not feel anything. He tried all pockets of his suit but was all in vain. He was shocked at how it went missing from his pockets. He even checked his briefcase in case he put it in unconsciously but nothing could be seen. He was sure he left the wallet in his back pocket

Looking back to where he came from, there was nothing he could see. His heart started to pound faster; his passport, tickets and ID cards were all in the wallet. If they were lost he would be lost too because this was his first time in Australia and he did not know his way around.

He quickly withdrew from the queue to the desk and ran back exactly the same track they entered the terminal from the bus in case he might have dropped it unknowingly while rushing to the checkout point. There was still nothing he could see.

When he got to where the bus dropped them off, there was a bus parking there. The door was opened and he just got in and headed straight to the seat number he was seated.

'Excuse me, what are you looking for?', asked the driver

'My wallet, sir.'

'What's your flight Number?'

'QF554'

'Oh, no! That bus has gone. This bus is for QF555.'

Timbo stood still; his heart froze and was on the verge of crying.

'Don't worry', the driver offered some comfort. *'If that driver finds it, he will hand it in the office. Just go back to the people at the desk and explain the situation; they will help you out'.*

'Thank you sir', he acknowledged the advice and slowly alighted the bus.

The time for his connecting flight was getting closer and he had to run back to the check-in desk to sort something out now that his passport had definitely gone missing from his pocket. He was the last person in the queue

'Excuse me madam', he asked the lady at the desk.

'Yes dear. What can I do for you',

'I've lost my wallet; my ticket for my connecting flight is in it and I don't know what to do if you can help me please', he begged.

'Sure. What's your name?

She typed his name into the computer as he quoted it. *'Oh yes. Your flight has just left and that was the last flight as well.'*

Timbo felt weak and numb. He was of the thought that he would be deported home because of no passport. He tried his best to be stoic and keep his balance.

'What about my luggage?', he queried.

'It's gone in the same flight', he was told

'Oh no', he sighed as he tried to compose himself. *'Will I be deported back home now that I've lost my passport?',* he enquired nervously.

The lady cheered as she tried to explain the procedure. *'No, you've already checked into the country, you do not need any passport to travel anywhere in the country. You can sleep in a hotel tonight and come back tomorrow and hopefully someone would find your wallet and hand it in. These things happen and are always handed in when they are found because they are not of any much use to anyone but you',* she enlightened his insecurity.

Before she continued he told her, *'Someone was supposed to meet me at the airport on the last flight. Can you please contact them that I will be coming tomorrow?'.*

He went on to say, *'This is my first time in Sydney. I have no knowledge of how to get to the nearest hotel and back to the airport if you can organise one for me please.'*

The lady nodded as she toyed with her keyboard. *'Sure. I can do that',* she answered calmly. *'I've booked you into this hotel which has a courtesy transport service to and from the hotel. It will be here in the next ten minutes and drop you here tomorrow at 9.00 am. You have a good sleep and enjoy your breakfast tomorrow before we see you again. But don't panic you'll get your wallet when we see you tomorrow',* she reassured him.

'Thanks a lot. You've been a great help', he complied

As he withdrew from the desk he was surprised to be met by the driver of the courtesy service.

'Hi, Are you Mr Aristo?', he asked Timbo.

'Yes.'

'*I'm Stein, I'm here to take you to the hotel*', he introduced himself. Before Timbo said anything more, the driver picked up his briefcase and led him to the car. He even opened the door for Timbo.

Timbo was very impressed with the service he had been accorded not only by the driver but also the ground flight attendants. It quickly diffused his stress over his lost wallet.

This was even more alleviated by the sparkling luster of the street lights and the splendour of the hotel. His jetlag and hunger were all but gone when leaning over the window and scanned the beauty of the city through its colourful lights. He retreated to his bed and tried to recall the day's upheavals until he could not think or open his eyes anymore.

When Timbo woke up the following morning, the lights, the radio and the television in the room were still on. He remembered being told at the airport to report back in the following morning to check if someone would hand in lost wallet. He looked at the clock, he had only slept for two hours but he felt as if he slept the whole night.

Just before he went for a shower, the telephone rang. '*Hello*', he answered in wonder who would ring him at such an early time.

'*Good morning sir. This is the receptionist reminding you that your transport for the airport will be ready in the next fifteen minutes*', answered the lady on duty.

'*Thank you*', Timbo was amazed at the efficiency of the service and in particular the courtesy of calling him sir. He could not recall organising a time for his return to the airport; he thought it could be the airport lady when she booked him in for the night. He wasted no time having a quick shower.

Timbo had no experience of a hotel before. Skimming the shower first, he noticed various small bottles and a couple of mini soap bars. He sniffed them all out of curiosity and realised they must be some sort of shower aloes.

He came from a tropical island where the water was always at body temperature. Unaware of the hot and cold taps, he reached for one and turned, and shockingly it was icy cold. He reflexively jumped backward and stared at the water. Without reaching for the warm one, he just assumed that it was supposed to be like that. He knew he was running out of time and thus endured a quick cold one.

It was exactly fifteen minutes after the receptionist called when someone knocked at the door. When he opened the door, it was the hotel attendant, '*Your cab is waiting sir. I'm here to take your luggage*', informed the attendant. The attendant noted that Timbo was still shivering; he did not know Timbo just had an icy cold shower.

'*Are you alright sir?*', the attendant asked.

'*Oh yes, I just had a cold shower*', assured Timbo. The attendant did not press further thinking it was Timbo's choice to have a cold shower.

'*So do you have any luggage to take down?*'

'*I only have a briefcase*', he answered.

'*I'll take that for you*', returned the attendant as he reached for it.

'*Thanks*', Timbo conceded. When they got to the waiting vehicle, the driver was already waiting with door opened for him. His crave for breakfast was nothing compared to the awesome VIP treatment he was accorded.

When reporting to the airline desk again for any news of his lost wallet, '*I'm sorry mate, we still haven't received any news of your wallet or your passport*', declared the officer.

'*So what shall I do then?*', Timbo asked in earnest.

'*Have you had breakfast yet?*', she asked.

'*No, and I'm not hungry*', he added.

'*I can see you are still worried about your passport. I suggest you go for something to eat now while we are waiting and hopefully someone might turn up with your wallet by the time you return. People have just started coming to work and most do not start until 9.00a.m.*', she urged him.

After breakfast there was still no sign of a wallet. The lady shook her head negatively when she saw Timbo again. However, she told him, '*You can still go to Melbourne if you want to pay for the next flight. You do not need a passport. They will reimburse you when you get down there. Your wallet, especially your passport, will also be sent down when its handed in*'.

Luckily, Timbo had divided his cash into both his pocket and wallet. Thus, he had just enough left to pay for the next flight as advised. Upon arrival, he was following the rest of the passengers to the **'LUGGAGE PICK UP'** zone when the front desk officer walked straight to him and asked, *'Excuse me. Did you lose anything in Sydney airport?'*

'Yes, my wallet with my passport in it', he answered.

'Don't worry, it's coming in the next flight; it will be here in half an hour.'

'Thank you, sir.'

'No problem. By the way, this is the message for you', the officer added.

'Thanks'. It was a phone number to call for a lift from the airport. Before making a call, he chased after the officer, *'Excuse me sir, my luggage came in my connecting flight last night. Where can I pick them up from?'* he asked.

'Follow me', the officer directed him to the baggage claims desk and was given there.

After calling the number given, the liaison officer arrived in less than fifteen minutes. *'G'day, I'm Sam. How are you?'* he greeted Timbo.

'Hi Sam, I'm Timbo. Thanks for coming. I'm sorry if I kept you waiting last night', he tried to smooth things out.

'Oh, no. I didn't come. The airline called my office so I knew in advance before the plane arrived. We better go now', he continued.

'Can we wait for my wallet? It's coming in the next flight. They said it's due in the next half an hour'.

'Don't worry. I will pick it up for you but you need to have a rest after all the troubles you've had. Let's go', the officer insisted as he led the way out.

The officer did not just drop Timbo off at the hotel, but he even made sure Timbo was comfortable with the place, *'I'll be back tomorrow morning to pick you up and we'll go to the main office. You have a good rest'.*

'Thank you, sir', he showed deep appreciation before he left.

On the following morning, a different driver turned up and took him to the office in the city. He was surprised to be met at the door by the officer who picked him up the day before with his wallet. He could not believe the recovery of his wallet with everything intact and the efficiency in the execution of the services.

'*Thank you, sir*', he hailed him

'*It's a pleasure*', he replied and left.

The Predecessor

While Timbo was waiting to see the officer in charge of overseas students, the driver who picked him earlier turned up again with another student. '*Hi, this is Jai*', he introduced the new arrival. '*Hello, I'm Timbo*', he introduced himself as they shook each other's hand.

'*I'll leave you two here; someone will call you shortly. Good luck for your studies and enjoy your stay*', the driver offered before leaving.

'*So it's nice to see you*', started Jai.

'*Yeah, nice to see you too*', joined Timbo.

'*Is this your first time here?*' asked Jai.

'*Yes. How about you?*'

'*No. I came here four years ago for secondary school teaching. I'm now back for 'Special Education.'*'

'*For what?*', he inquired

'*For the education of children with special needs*', Jai explained.

'*Oh that's good; you know the place well then and you can be my guide*', Timbo confessed humourously.

'*What are you here for?*', asked Jai.

'*To complete the advanced radiography course I started back in your country*'.

'That's nice to know. We can only be thankful to these countries for helping us out financially and academically. Otherwise our countries will never advance to another level', confessed Jai

'Or we'll never be able to see this side of the world too or even meet you', added Timbo wittily.

Timbo glanced at his watch. It was exactly 9.00 o'clock when they saw the lady coming over and took them in to the office. *'Hello, I'm Nancy. I'll be your person of contact while you are here'*, she introduced herself.

'How are you finding your first days?' she asked them both in general as a goodwill gesture

'Ok thanks', answered Jai.

She turned to Timbo, *'I'm sorry to hear about your troubles. Have you got everything back?*

'Yes thanks', Timbo responded happily.

'That's good. You'll probably have more to pick up not only your studies but also the place because this is your first time. Jai should be ok he was here before', she commented with a smile.

'Oh yes. I'll be his tour guide', Jai joked to ease the formality.

When released for lunch, Jai told Timbo, *'We won't go into a restaurant, it's expensive. We'll just buy takeaways.'*

Timbo agreed. He did not know much of a difference but followed Jai's guidance. *'We'll just go window shopping now because there's not enough time but we'll go in when we are finished this afternoon'*, advised Jai.

Timbo did not show any emotions while window shopping but he definitely was taken aback with the rainbow fluorescence of the building lights inside and outside. He did not know where to look because everything was a marvel to him.

Thus he almost jumped when Jai tapped him on the shoulder, *'Let's go, it's time now.'*

It was a full day of information to absorb. But Timbo took them all in excitement. It was even more sensational when they were guided to the bank nearby to open their savings accounts to deposit their first stipends. It was the last task for them to do before the end of the day.

'Enjoy your stay and best of luck for the studies. Feel free to call me anytime you need my help', she concluded the day when leaving the bank.

'*We will. Many thanks for your time and help'*, responded Jai as they shook hands to part.

By the end of the week Timbo learnt that Jai was a middle aged married man. Timbo was not quite sure if Jai was a school principal or a senior respected teacher before he came. But he seemed a smart person to be sent again while there were hundred others, especially single ones, in his teaching field.

Timbo on the other hand was single and in his late teen. Thus, Timbo did not only look at Jai as a guide but also as a father to him.

On their first night out, Timbo noticed his friend Jai was a very smart pool table player. They went from pub to pub without spending a cent on any drinks but he would challenge the winner to play for a jug of beer. By the time they would leave, their table had already been filled with full jugs. Jai was only sipping as he played while Timbo held onto a soft drink.

Timbo thought it would be annoying to those he challenged because they weren't being used. Jai did not care. He would just signal to Timbo to go to the next pub whenever he felt like it.

The night was getting late and Jai did not appear willing to call it. He was still enjoying himself. Timbo on the other hand was dying to leave. He was not only new to such a life but fearful of their safety at such time of the night. But he did not want to wreck their first night by leaving early. Thus, he persevered a bit longer for Jai's sake until 2.00 o'clock in the morning. He finally had the courage to tell Jai, '*Sorry mate, but I can't go on. I'm tired'*.

'*I can see that my friend'*, agreed Jai. '*Don't worry about me. I'll hang out a bit longer but we'll get a cab for you'*.

When they got to the cab, Jai did not only tell the driver the destination but also paid for the taxi.

'*Ok my friend, I'll see you tomorrow'*, he farewelled Timbo.

'*Take care of you too*', warned Timbo as the taxi left.

Timbo did not hear from his friend the next day and he was worried. Anything could have happened and he did not have a clue on how to find him, alive or dead. It was not until after dinner that he heard a knock. Jai entered excitedly while Timbo looked on in disbelief, '*Man, I was scared to death of your whereabouts when I did not hear from you after lunch*', he admitted. '*What time did you come back?*'

'*Now*', Jai answered cheerily. He did not seem perturbed with Timbo's concern.

'*What! My goodness . What have you been doing the whole night?*' Timbo kept pressing but Jai just laughed as if he could not believe the night he had. '*So you were just retracing your footprints from the last time you were here?*' he joshed

'*You know what*', Jai could not hold his excitement any longer, '*This bird challenged me in the pool table and she beat me twice*'.

'*What! you lost in the pool games?*', Timbo reaffirmed. '*I can't believe that after watching you sweeping through the challengers last night. Anyway?*', he prompted Jai.

'*I told her I did not have the money to buy her the jugs but offered myself jokingly, and that's why I'm late back*', Jai revealed naively.

'*A HA. So there you are, sowing your seeds and here am I worrying about you*', he laughed as they tried to settle down.

'*Well, you know, being a family man miles away from a wife and kids is tough, very tough. You will remember me for this when you get to it too. That's why it's hard for me to come to a hotel room, it's very depressing*', Jai professed. '*Its either keeping busy with studies or be entertained to take my mind off them*'.

'*I see, that's very true*', Timbo conceded. It had just clicked on him why his friend kept hanging out when he was dying to return the previous night. '*But playing pool and enjoying the music should be more than enough, but not bedding someone else. Don't you think so?*', he challenged Jai.

'*As I said, when you get to this stage, you'll take anything that will heal the pain*', Jai seemed to be giving Timbo a lecture for the years ahead. Their chat was interrupted when they heard over the hotel intercom, '*Calling Jai, phone call for you please*'.

'*We'll talk later. It must be my wife*', he left immediately.

'*Let me talk to her first so I can tell her where you were last night*', teased Timbo as his friend ran to take the call in his room.

Timbo thought he had finally found someone open enough to share the life with, and old enough to guide him for his time of study.

The advent of the new Study life

The reality of the new life had finally arrived on the first day in lectures. Timbo was on his own then and he had to find his way around to get to lectures. This was his first time in such a massive multistorey complex. His only guidance was to scan the directory at the main entrance for his lecture room and follow directions.

He knew he was late to the lecture but pressed on to ascertain his confidence for the next time. When he eventually got to the door, he stealthily opened it, sneaked in and took the first seat available from behind where the entry was, thinking it was his unit. But after a couple of minutes, he realised it was a different unit.

The lecturer kept babbling without taking heed of what the students were doing. Likewise, students weren't even bothered. There were those concentrating on listening, some were taking notes, while others were knitting.

He slowly got up and tiptoed out without distracting them all. Upon double checking the directory, he found out that it was the same room number but different floor. It was getting far too late to enter again and thus, he decided to skip it to give him time to study the building directories thoroughly and getting to know their locations physically for next lectures.

The following day was his first day in the allocated hospital. It was just as big as the school building he attended the day before. Finding his way to the X-ray Department was not a problem. However on his way out after hours, he could not figure out where he was heading to until he ended up in the Mental Health Ward.

Timbo thought he was heading out until a patient walked over to him and said hello. He was joined by another and another until he was physically surrounded by patients. He tried to go back the way he entered but there was no space for him to move. Luckily, the nurse on duty saw him and called, *'Are you alright?'*

'No. I'm on my way out but I think I'm lost', admitted Timbo hoping desperately she would relieve him of all these patients.

'Come this way', she signalled him to follow.

Closing the door behind the patients, she whispered, *'This is the Mental Ward. Did you know it?'*, she asked.

'No. I'm new to the hospital', he admitted.

'I can see. So now you know. Try and avoid it next time because they keep going and going once they get you', she warned.

She opened the door for him, *'Thanks a lot'*.

'You're welcomed, take care'.

Homesickness

It had been three months since his arrival in Australia, but Timbo had not met or heard of anyone from his tribe in the school or hospital. He had met many other nationalities but not his. His excitement over seeing the new place started to fade.

Jai's statement when they were in the hotel began to become a reality. His room was becoming a depressing niche since his friend left for his institute of study. He had no one to share his life with let alone the jokes. He was getting homesick. He wanted to see or speak to someone from his country.

He remembered Nancy, the sponsored students' liaison officer. Her final word outside the bank before she left was to contact her for anything they might need. Thus he eventually called her, *'Hello, this is Nancy'*,

'Hi Nancy, this is Timbo. I'm one of the sponsored students you are looking after', he introduced himself.

'*Yes, that's correct. How are you?*' she confirmed his call.

'*I'm fine thanks.*'

'*What can I help you for?*' she diplomatically asked.

'*I'm sorry to bother you but I'm just wondering if there was another student from my country you are sponsoring I can talk to please?*' he asked.

'*Are you getting homesick?*' she jokingly asked.

'*That's right*', he disclosed.

'*Oh, you poor thing, I'm not surprised. You are not the only one. Most of the students we sponsor go through the same stage. I'll try and find out. Can I call you back later?*', she reassured.

'*Sure.*'

'*Ok. Leave it with me but you take care of yourself*', she comforted him.

Two hours later, Timbo received a call from Nancy, '*Hi Timbo, it's Nancy from the Australian sponsoring department,* she introduced herself.

'*Hello Nancy, How are you?*', he responded.

'*I'm fine thank you*', she answered. '*Look I have found one of your country mates*'.

'*Really?*', Timbo interjected excitedly.

'*Yes, but I could not call him until I have you permission to give him your number so he can call you. Do you allow me to give him your phone number?*', she asked.

'*Please yes*', he unconditionally acquiesced.

'*Good. His name is Jose. I will contact him then and you expect a call from him in the near future*', she reassured him before they hung up.

A week passed and there was no phone call. Timbo's excitement started to wave. He had every faith in Nancy's word but the fact that no one called made him wonder if his country mate had the same homesickness feeling like him or was he enjoying his time away from home. Either way, Timbo yearned that hopefully Jose would eventually call him somehow.

Timbo was busy in sorting films in the department's filing room when he heard his name over the deparment's intercom, *'Phone call for Timbo please'*. he dropped everything and ran for the nearest phone. He knew very well this could be from Jose as expected. But to his surprise, it was his old mate Jai, *'Hey, How are you? Nice to hear from you again'*, he greeted Jai.

Jai was laughing loudly as usual as he returned the greetings. The conversation was starting to gain momentum when Timbo felt a tap on his shoulder, *'There's another call for you'*, whispered his classmate. He tried to cut short the phone talk but Jai kept going and going because it had been two months since they last met.

By the time they hung up, Timbo's other caller had gone already. Timbo's feelings were in a total tangle. He was excited to hear Jai again after a while but regretted missing the other caller who could be Jose, or Nancy, the only ones who knew his phone number.

Without giving up hope, Timbo thought Jose would try again if he really was searching for him. When he was called again, Timbo was definitely positive it could be Jose's. As soon as he heard Jose's voice over the phone, he was thrilled. It was even more comforting to hear him speaking their dialect. They went on and on as if they left home together. When he hung up, the place was almost empty. The staff had already gone home.

It was very weird for him to hear that after all these three solid months of English speaking. This, he thought, could be the good cause for compulsory English speaking rule back in his selective school time. A thing he was very critical about but now appreciated the beauty of such vision.

The Fostering Leaf of the Sponsorship Package

While Timbo was still vacillating between his studies and the cultural shock; he totally forgot the fostering part of his sponsorship package. When Nancy called to inform him of their meeting with foster families, he asked, *'What's that?'*

'It's part of our sponsoring package where Australian families volunteer to support overseas students so they would appreciate their stay and have a better understanding of a typical Australian family life', she explained.

'That sounds nice', he admired. *'How does it work?'* he enquired.

'*This meeting is an introductory one so you get to know your family and vice versa. After that they will organize a combined activity with other families and their students. This will give you a chance to meet other sponsored students and their families*', she elaborated on the package. '*Is that alright with you?*' she confirmed.

'*Oh yes, it's very thoughtful of you with such a programme*', he voiced his gratitude.

'*Good. Your foster family, Mr and Mrs Richardson, will call you on the day they will come and see you and organize everything I mentioned for you. But do not be scared to contact me if you are not comfortable with anything*', she encouraged him.

'*I will and many thanks for your unyielding support,*' he complimented her service.

On Wednesday morning, he was paged for a phone call. It was from the father of the foster family. '*Hello it's Timbo.*'

'*Hello, this is Richard Richardson. I'm your foster father while you are in Australia*'.

'*Hello Mr Richardson, how are you?*' Timbo greeted his foster father.

'*I'm fine thanks. I'm calling to organize a day and a place where we can meet up. How about this Friday after hours?*' he asked.

'*That's fine with me*', Timbo answered anxiously.

'*Shall we meet you at the Coffee Shop adjacent to the waiting foyer?*' Mr Richardson tried to corroborate.

'*That sounds good. I'll see you then and many thanks for calling*', confirmed Timbo. He had mixed feelings; he was excited at the idea but nervous of meeting his foster family. He was scared he might do something normal in his culture but offensive to theirs.

When he got to the foyer as agreed with Mr Richardson, there was no one there but a group of paramedics who were helping someone to the emergency room. He wanted to help but there was no space for him to squeeze in. Thus, he decided to stick to the meeting plan and waited for Mr Richardson.

He then realised that he forgot his jacket in the X-ray room he had worked in earlier and decided to run back for it to be back in time. The X-ray area was packed with patients when he got there. He had no option but tried to help out. To his surprise, he came across Mr Richardson's request form. He hadn't met him before but the name rang a bell.

After the introduction and X-ray examination, the patient's wife asked Timbo, *'Do you mind if I ask a question?'*

'No, not at all', he willingly responded.

'Have you been working here long?' she asked.

'Oh, I'm only a student. I've only been here a couple of months', he flatly avowed.

'I'm sorry if I'm too intrusive', she apologized.

'Oh no, it's ok', he intervened.

'I'm Mrs Richardson and this is my husband, we were meant to meet a student named Timbo after hours', she tried to confirm. *'But he had a sudden sharp chest pain and was rushed into the emergency room without knowing he would end up here, and that's why I'm asking you if you are the one'*, she tried to explain Timbo.

Timbo gave her a respectful smile and gave a compromising response, *'Yes madam, I'm sorry for what happened but I'm glad to meet you though it shouldn't be in this condition'*, he tried to comfort them.

'Oh no, it's no one's fault but what a way to meet', she jokingly commented. *'It's nice to meet you and welcome to Australia'*, she offered a hospitable hand.

'Thanks and nice meeting you too', reiterated Timbo.

While still waiting for the porter to push Richard back, Timbo decided to do it himself as a token of respect for their kind consideration in coming to see him. By the time they got to the Emergency room, they were conversing like old friends. Before Timbo left, the Richardsons reminded Timbo that they would be back to pick him up for the overseas students and their foster families' get together on the Saturday fortnight.

'Many thanks for your help', Mrs Richardson voiced her appreciation to Timbo.

'Thanks for your kindness too and sorry for his troubles. Hope he gets better soon', he offered some comforting words before he left.

'Not to worry; he'll get better; he's a tough man. Aren't you dear?' she acclaimed him while farewelling Timbo.

'Take care of yourself too. It was nice meeting you. We'll see you in a fortnight's time', she concluded as he left them.

When he got back to the department, he was shocked to be blown by the staff on duty. *'You should never push that patient back regardless of whether or not you know him',* she blasted. *'The porters are the only ones legally recruited to do it; if anything happens they are responsible for it'.*

Timbo was off guard. He did not know his next move other than apologising. *'I'm sorry; I was only trying to help'.*

'I know but it is in your best interest to avoid other people's responsibilities. I have nothing personal against you but to protect you from unforeseen mishaps', she said as she slowly calmed down.

Timbo wanted to disappear from hereafter but she was busy. He decided to put up with her and kept helping until the workload was cleared.

'You are late home', she commented in a more compromising tone.

'It's ok. It's Friday I don't have to come in tomorrow', he swiped her concern.

'You better go; thanks for your help. Don't think otherwise of what I said earlier but always cover your back all the time', she warned.

'Thanks for the advice. I'll remember it. You have a goodnight too and see you next week', he absorbed the finale of the week as he left for home.

The Training Highlights

Upon starting in the new hospital, he could not differentiate between students and qualified staff. They all looked efficient during the execution of the service. It was only when he went to lectures after hours that he started to identify the students from the qualified staff. He was very impressed with the students' efficiencies. It was even more inspiring because of the indiscriminate atmosphere within the department. Everyone was treated equally. And he admired it greatly.

After his first week, a staff meeting was held and he was shocked to be honoured with a welcome word from the professor heading the department. He felt very humbled to be offered such an honour amongst a professional crowd.

The next day, he was asked over the phone by the hospital's Public Relations department for an interview, not for job, but for information purposes since he was the first student recruit from the pacific region.

He agreed to it and was scheduled for the afternoon of the following day.

When the time came, he noted that the interviewer was a blind man. He never thought such people could be employed. He recalled the only blind man back home who could read but only when preaching in church but not employed fulltime like this interviewer.

When they were in the interview room, the interviewer started, '*Good day Timbo, I'm Peter Koolash. I work for the hospital's Public Relations department. The interview is mainly to get some feedback from you regarding your experience in the hospital so that we can improvise our service to foreign recruits especially students like you. Is that alright with you?*' he asked Timbo's approval.

'*Yes sir*', answered Timbo in a very quiet and timid voice.

'*Are you scared?*' the Public relations officer asked Timbo.

'*No sir.*'

'*But?*'

'*It's just that I'm not used to being interviewed like this*', Timbo explained as he tried to hide his emotions.

'*Good. It shouldn't be long*', he was assured.

The officer was right. It was the shortest interview Timbo had been through. It did not last five minutes and Timbo was very happy with it.

The only questions he was asked were about his field of study, his attitude towards the atmosphere in the hospital and his future aspirations. He was surprised to be told it was over. He was also amazed at the officer's manner in which he conducted the interview; he was relaxed, and very welcoming to Timbo.

Miscommunication

Timbo was rostered from one area of specialty to another like any other student for their clinical competency training. If the specialty was not available in the hospital he was based, he would be sent to another hospital offering the service. When he entered the cardiac suite, he was briefed on the importance of strictly adhering to the sterile culture of the room especially during the procedure to prevent infection. Thus, everyone involved in the procedure had to change into hospital gowns, shoe covers, masks and head caps. Everything had to be double checked and it was imperative that he did it too.

Timbo was told by his supervising radiographer that the radiologist, who interprets and reports on the procedure, would count one to three and the radiographer pressed on the X-ray button until he called to stop. He was warned that there would be some point of time the radiologist would tell the patient to cough repeatedly. Timbo nodded as briefed and agreed to observe the first case.

In the second one, Timbo was given a go. He tried nervously to remember and follow all he was told. The noise from the staff of different specialties talking behind him seriously impaired his hearing while trying desperately to listen to the performing specialist's call from the mask. Thus, when the doctor called the patient, *'Cough, cough, cough'*, he reflexively took his finger from the button and hence stopped the procedure prematurely.

'What happened?' the specialist enquired thinking that there was something wrong with the machine.

'I'm sorry. I thought you called, 'Stop, stop, stop'. He apologised. He turned to his supervisor, *'I'm sorry but I could not hear clearly through his mask and the noise behind'.*

'It's ok. Don't panic. I know it's not easy trying to listen to someone talking through the mask while others are talking. Try again, but just try your best', his supervisor sympathised.

'*We're ready when you are*', he called the specialist. The procedure started again with Timbo still in control and the supervising radiographer by his side this time, repeating the call for Timbo's clarity. The second run was a success for Timbo and he was relieved.

'*Good. Now you can do it*', commended his supervisor. Timbo reciprocated in great relief, '*Many thanks for your guidance*'.

He went home with mixed feelings. Concerned he was letting his supervisor down and grateful for his supervisor's patient guidance.

Back to muscles

On the next day, Timbo was exposed to a different procedure; it was for the examination of blood flow in the lower body, from the hips to the toes. He was again informed on its management and how it related to the rest of the body.

Timbo just nodded and watched as his supervisor actually demonstrated his supposed role. Images were taken in a set time sequence while the table and the patient move synchronously. Unexpectedly, the table stopped moving. The supervisor's short term fixes were all exhausted unsuccessfully. But the examination had to be completed. Thus, he turned to Timbo, '*We'll continue in the old way using the old table*'.

Timbo did not know the alternative but just followed his supervisor. '*This old table has a sliding board on rollers. I want you to pull from one end according to my count until finished. Is that ok with you*', he confirmed with Timbo.

'*Sure*', Timbo assured.

After a quick run through, he put on a radiation protection gown and glasses, and a neck cover, before holding the board end for pulling. The supervisor repeated the procedure again to ascertain clarity before continuing.

The nurse signaled readiness with thumbs up, '*Ready Timbo?*' called the supervisor.

Timbo just nodded and started pulling as soon as he heard the call, '*One, two, three, pull, one two, one two three pull, one two three pull, one two, one two three, stop*'.

Timbo was sweating furiously like running a marathon. It was not only the outpouring of the exercise with weights of his protective gears, but also the fear of making another mistake like the '*Coughing case*'.

When the films came out they were just as good as the failed modern equipment. He was more than exuberant, and so was his supervisor. '*We may as well throw that new expensive equipment in the bin*', scoffed his supervisor. Timbo just hung his gown with a smile and helped with transferring the patient onto his bed.

His supervisor tapped Timbo on the shoulder as a complimentary gesture. It made his day.

Home again: The Harvest Time

When Timbo returned home and started working in his home country's main hospital, the government was building a new hospital. He never thought much of it until he was unexpectedly asked his opinion on the layout of the new X-ray department.

It was a test, Timbo recognised, of reaping any fruits from what he was sent for. He was quick to apply the knowledge he learnt from his studies and the departmental layout in the X-ray departments he was exposed to during his studies – all without referring to a textbook. He was grateful he was being asked his opinion when he was still fresh from his studies so he could contribute constructively.

Timbo remembered distinctly one of the questions in his final exam was the critiquing of different X-ray department layouts. Thus, he did not only draft one when asked, but was also able to justify his opinions on such a layout. He was glad he could contribute to his country's development as a favour for sending him overseas for further studies.

Timbo tried to evolve into the new working culture of his home country. He found it a bit different if not great. It was carefree and more relaxed. However, he was starting to realise that he was referred to every now and then for his opinion in many occasions.

It was very different to what he used to when studying where he had to rely on others for confirmation of any uncertainties or providing advice in the execution of the service. The responsibility was then on him; some officially, others unconsciously. He started to realise then that he had to live up to certain expectations too.

It was a big realization as that was why he was sent away for training. It was part of his country's development programme – just as the Medical Director briefed him when given the choice of fields of study on his first vacation back from studying.

On Call

Starting on call service was a novel lifestyle he had to adjust to. He had to respond and attend regardless of the time of the day or night. It was a pledge he made before he took up the course.

One night, he was called in and was stunned when he was given a dead body for an X-ray examination. This was his first exposure to such cases. Once the cover sheet was removed, he felt an electric chill numbing his body. He could not say a word. It reminded him of their first practical lesson in school. The lecturer took them to the section of the laboratory where the dead bodies were preserved in the 44 gallon drums filled with preservative liquid.

The lecturer had called them closer to the drum he was standing. No one suspected anything until the lecturer reached down the murky fluid and lifted out an arm and hand all intact. Everyone was taken aback but the lecturer was just laughing at their surprises.

Likewise, their body languages told it all. He looked at the porter bringing the body as if to say, *'Why did you bring this?'*. The porter just shrugged his shoulder indicating, *'I'm only doing what I'm told to do'*.

Without saying a word, Timbo picked up the request X-ray form and stepped out of the room as if he was trying to reconfirm the request, but he was trying to regroup himself from such an unexpected case. When he entered again, the porter had sneaked out the other door. That left him alone with the dead body. It was then that he really felt scared even though the lights were glaring at them.

When he exit again looking for the porter, he almost dropped dead by the sudden appearance of the porter from the corner. *'Wholly shit'*, he blared. *'You scared me to death'*, he admitted in a choking tone.

The porter just smiled and joined him into the room. *'I knew you were scared this being your first time. I've been here too long and have seen many of these'*, the porter confided in Timbo. Timbo kept the conversation alive to diffuse his fear while doing the examination. When Timbo finished, *'I'm done.'* He said. *'Thanks for the company. He's all yours'*, he told the porter.

'No worries. You'll get used to this', added the porter as he wheeled the bed away.

Timbo did not stay long after they left. The place seemed haunted all over and had to leave as soon as he could. It made him wonder if this was the right job for him. It was an experience that challenged his ego this time.

Timbo's Social Life Changes

It did not take long for Timbo to work after returning home from his studies when he got married. He knew he had to one day not too early and not too late. If he rushed through or left it too late he might make a mistake that would traumatise him for good.

Some senior members of his staff even advised him to marry a non-local to avoid local complexities. However, he remembered from the Psychology unit he studied that people from the same background coexist well with the least discord than those with different backgrounds. Timbo ended up marrying a former teacher trainee he used to pass to and from schools. His forward thinking was that her teaching experience would be a helping asset should they be blessed with kids in the future.

After the wedding, Timbo was ready to settle without any thoughts of leaving his country largely because some of his family members including his father had passed away during the time he was away. Moreover, he wanted to serve his country in return for the opportunity he was given to pursue his dream.

However, an unexpected visit took a turn. When his wife's New Zealand residential status was on the verge of expiry, they thought to try if it could be renewed at the local High Commissioner's office. It was on the day of expiry they had an appointment with the High Commissioner. After skimming through both their passports, Timbo was shocked when the High Commissioner asked, *'So when are you planning to travel?* .

Quick-wittedly, Timbo gave an unplanned answer, '*As soon as we are given the approval*'.

Without further questions, they were given a *Clearance Form* to be signed by the designated departments and to be returned whenever it was done. They left the office in disbelief at the outcome. This was unexpected; they had only gone in for the renewal of his wife's residential status in case they might want to go for a holiday sometime later but not this early. But the opportunity was at hand. Timbo and his wife realized they had to reassess their situation on whether or not to take it.

After a week, things had finally sunk in. In his mind, if he took the opportunity he was given earlier for his studies, he would be selfish if he denied his family, especially his children, this opportunity. Thus he made up his mind to take the offer. He believed he had served enough years to reciprocate the government's post academic agreement.

Whilst there was no definite accommodation or employment organised for them in New Zealand, Timbo and his wife planned to book into a motel as a starting point until either of them got a job. The dream was to eventually get into a house of their own. Timbo surmised that they were financially sufficient for a few months until they settled in their new destination.

The only hurdle in their plan was his mother. He had made a pledge to look after her after his father's death but things had now changed unexpectedly that diffused such allegiance. However, his mother was a forward thinker and understanding. They would not proceed with their plan if she did not give her blessing after being informed of it.

Bruises of the Unexpected

Upon arrival at the Auckland airport, there was no one awaiting them because of their motel plan. Timbo was not aware they were travelling together with his wife's cousin. When the cousin learnt they were heading for a motel, he strenuously discouraged Timbo from such a move and requested they join him at his sister's home. Timbo was adamant they stick with the original plan for the sake of their children.

His wife on the other hand was having some second thoughts and advised Timbo to go with her cousin in case their funds would dry up sooner before either of them could find a job. It was only then that Timbo finally acquiesced. He was not that happy with the change of plan but he was also aware of his culture and tradition that it would be rude to turn down an invitation.

When they arrived at the house, the cousin's sister and her husband were obviously taken by surprise. Nothing was prepared like food, beddings etc. Thus it almost took the whole night to cook a meal for them all. By the time dinner was ready Timbo's children were fast asleep. It was only then that Timbo learnt that the cousin who invited them for the stay did not live there but had to leave the following morning for the south island.

Timbo was annoyed with the cousin as he had only agreed in the last minute to the invitation thinking he was to be their host. But now he was departing and leaving them stranded with strangers they never met before.

On the following night, the host lady was taken to the emergency doctor for treatment. It was a sudden medical onset which Timbo thought it stemmed from the stress of hosting them unexpectedly.

On the second night a similar episode occured, this time it was a bit more serious. From then on, she would be fine at daytime but got hysterically feverish at night. The husband ended up calling in sick the following day and consequently the whole week. Thus began a pattern of absence every night after dinner; the couple would leave home and spend the whole night searching for a 'spiritual' witch doctor.

In the next morning, Timbo noticed the lady's bruised face. Upon enquiry, they told him it was the result of the treatment she had from the 'spiritual' doctor. When they explained the treatment, it sounded like exorcism to Timbo. The witch doctor used the bible to hit the lady's face to ward off the devil.

'But she is very bruised; he must have really hit her very hard, Didn't he?', queried Timbo.

'The witch doctor indicated that it was evidence of the treatment's usefulness', the husband answered. Timbo said no more.

Once they were not visiting the 'spiritual' doctor, Timbo and his family would hear a commotion about 4.00am at night. When Timbo and his wife popped outside to check on the problem, the husband just sat down saying, he was chasing out the devil that caused his wife's breathlessness. Timbo could not comprehend the obsession dominating this couple. They had been living in this country with a health service equivalent to those of technologically advanced countries and yet they were not utilising such avenues but resorting to unfounded conservative treatments.

The impact of the husband abstaining from work most of the days was creeping into Timbo and his wife financially. The husband was flagrantly requesting assistance for things like groceries, their baby's necessities, and petrol despite the fact they did not have time to look for jobs since their arrival. Timbo was getting worried their fund was starting to dry up faster than he had planned. Thus he told his wife they had to move out if they were to survive and, most importantly, to give them and their children some space.

But he had to find a place first without telling the couple. He left home early the following morning to go apartment hunting. The idea was to be settled first in order to avoid being stranded financially before he and his wife could land a job.

When the lady's sickness subsided Timbo and his wife sat down with her after breakfast and surprised her with the news they were moving out that day. They knew if they told her the day before, her sickness would have been triggered and thus prevented their departure. Coincidentally, Timbo's brother in law turned up to see them, and therefore used his van to move their things to the new apartment.

When settling in their own apartment for the first time, they felt as if they just arrived in New Zealand. There was no time for celebration or house warming as the need for jobs drove them. Before they slept on their first night, Timbo and his wife made a plan to start taking turns looking for jobs the following morning. Timbo would start in the morning while his wife looked after the children, and, vice versa in the afternoon.

When his wife was late home on the second afternoon, from job searching, Timbo had some mixed feelings; she was either lost because they were new to the area, or, probably got some luck with a job. They had a three month baby who was still breastfeeding then. When she cried, Timbo resorted to the orange juice he manually extracted into the bottle to feed her to allay her hunger until his wife arrived.

It was dusk and raining when Timbo's wife arrived home. As soon as Timbo saw a hand of green bananas and a bottle of milk with her, he knew she had the luck with some sort of job. *'Are we getting some new luck with you buying those things?'* he enthused.

'I'm sorry dear for being late', she apologised. *'I did have some trial run with the sewing machine before I came. When I initially asked the boss, he rejected me straightaway but when I showed him my qualifications he immediately changed his tone and said, "Oh we are looking for people like you". But that was just after he rejected me. So, as soon as he offered me the job, I asked him to give me a machine so I can have quick run through before starting tomorrow'.*

'If our funds were not critical, you could have easily told him to shove his job after rejecting you initially. That's blatant lying', he criticised empathetically for his wife's behalf. *'But we'll just take it for the time being until we are back to normal then you can look elsewhere. Thanks for the effort anyway.'* he cheered her.

Timbo and his wife had no watch or a radio to tell the time. Thus, when they heard shoe clanking outside in the middle of the night, they thought it was time to be ready for work. His wife was ready to start but dosed off to sleep again, after they found out from a passer-by outside it was only after 2.00 o'clock in the morning.

Until they bought a clock, Timbo's wife would regularly leave for work when the shoe clatters outside got more and more frequent as more people took to the street for work. It was the start of their working lives in New Zealand not only for his wife but also for Timbo as a fulltime carer for their children. A new experience, since their children were born.

Industrial Radiographer

Timbo always bought the newspaper from the nearest shop each morning to look for a job. Though his wife was working, he still believed it was a manly thing to feed his family. Moreover, his qualification would be wasted while in the prime of his life and career if he just sat around. After two weeks job searching, to his excitement, he came across an ad for an Industrial Radiographer. *'What's this, an industrial radiographer?',* he asked himself.

After calling to enquire for the role, he was told to attend an interview the following day. When his wife arrived home, *'I've got an interview tomorrow',* he elatedly declared.

'What for?', she responded anxiously.

'Industrial radiographer'.

'What's that?', she wondered.

'It's a radiographer of some sort. I'll find out tomorrow'.

'What about me?' she continued.

'What about you?' he repeated.

'I've just started in my job. Does that mean I'll quit it for the kids while you work?' she tried to justify the consequences of his interview.

'We'll see. If I get it, maybe we can sort something out but let me get through the first step first', he tried to pacify her.

She was not quite receptive but she knew they had to sort themselves out amicably for the sake of the kids.

'*So what time is your interview?*', she tried to be more diplomatic.

'*4.00p.m. I've pushed it to the latest time in order to match your finishing hour for the kids*', he said as he tried to convince her he was not being selfish in his motive but family inclusive in his desire to provide for his family.

When Timbo returned the following afternoon, he was overly excited. He hugged his wife and kids, '*I've struck a good deal dear*', he openly declared. '*You don't have to leave your job unless you want to*', he continued.

'*What do you mean?*' his wife was eager to know.

'*I've been offered the job but I managed to negotiate to start after you get home so the kids won't miss out*', he explained.

'*But we don't have a car for you when you finish at night*', his wife kept nagging him.

'*That's why I said earlier I've struck a good deal. I'll use the company car for work and come home with it and return in the following morning for the day shift workers. How cool is that?*' he asked rhetorically.

'*Oh that's nice of them*', she finally hailed his new job after seeing the light in her uncertainty.

'*What do you think?*', he asked ecstatically.

'*What makes an industrial radiographer different from the medical one?*', she still wanted to know.

'*Put it simply, a medical radiographer takes X-rays of patients while an industrial one takes X-rays of metals*', clarified Timbo.

'*AHHHH, I see*', she accepted.

'*Anything else?*' he enticed her.

She just shrugged her shoulders and smiled away.

'*You did not ask if there is any catch*', he tried to keep the excitement alive.

'*No, but is there any?*' she responded.

'*Yes, the car is manual but I only drive automatic ones. But, not to worry, I'll use it to teach myself to drive manually*', he tried to cheer her up. '*The main thing is that I've got a job without losing yours while both caring for the kids*'.

'*That's true*', approved his wife.

Fighting the Manual Car

When Timbo was late from work on the second night of work, his wife was in a panic. She would not know where to look for or even describe his appearance to the police if she called them as a missing person. She just curled up on the sofa and prayed furiously for his safety. She was just about to dose off to sleep when she was awoken by the knock at the door.

Timbo's wife did not run to it instantly but looked first through the glass if there was one or two people. If there were two, it would definitely be police. That would mean trouble and disaster to her and children. When she saw only one person she cautiously opened the door to make sure it was Timbo. Timbo was white as hell and in a frustrating mood.

'*I was worried. Why were you late?*', she enquired.

'*I'm sorry dear but I could not get the car going uphill when I stopped at the traffic lights. Cars behind me kept beeping their horns, others shouting, "You stupid thing. Get your shit out of the way". I was still struggling changing gears hoping madly one of them would push it forth until the red lights came up again*', he poured out his embarrassment. '*Luckily, there was no cop around*'.

'*So how did you get it going?*'.

'*Oh, I don't know. It was just a mere coincidence that it moved forward synchronously with green light again. Otherwise, I would spend the whole night there and could end up being ticketed by a cop if someone calls them*', he admitted in relief.

'*In that case, you really need proper manual driving lessons. You can't afford to go on like that; you may end up being hit from behind by some impatient driver, if not fined by the cops*', she warned.

'I agree. I'll try and get the company car over the weekend for practices until I get paid to fund professional driving lessons. But, don't panic, I'll get there', he cheered her up.

He did not have to ask for the company car because there were some works for him to be done over the weekend and thus had to use it after hours. He was working almost every weekend by this time and thus gave him more confidence in his driving skill and hence dispelled inclinations for professional training.

As Timbo got busier and their financial situation improved, Timbo and his wife reassessed their family situation again and eventually agreed for her to refrain from working in order to be at home fulltime with the kids. Timbo reverted to a day shift so they could be all together at the ends of the working days. The kids were happy too.

The Paper Mill

Easter break was a week away now and it was Timbo's family's first Easter abroad. They did not have any solid event planned for it other than relaxing. That was until his boss called him into the office before the end of that week. *'Look, there's a job going over the Easter weekend and I'm asking if you can do it for us'*, he politely approached Timbo.

Timbo was not so keen on doing the job because he was not only familiar with the location of the job but it was also their first Easter weekend since arrival. He was under the impression that there should be someone doing the job before they called.

'Was there anyone there before?' Timbo asked.

'Two of our boys that are based there will be going away for a break and that's why I'm asking if you can fill in. I thought you would be great at it.' he explained. Before Timbo gave an answer, the boss went on to say, *'The rate will be $25 an hour for 24 hours tax free for the whole time you will be there; everything else paid for'*.

'So what's involved if I may ask?' Timbo queried.

'They are building a new boiler for the Paper Mill. They want us to check five percent of the welding they are doing for any cracks and what not', explained the boss.

At this stage, Timbo and his wife had been working on their new house. They had yet to furnish it and put carpet in. They also had to pay their solicitor and the associated fees like insurance, connection fees for amenities like electricity and gas before they could move into it.

With this in mind, Timbo thought this new subcontract would be too good to pass up for their financial obligations when completed. Thus, he gave an impromptu positive response without consulting his wife.

Back at home, life continued as usual. The news of going away for the Easter break to work somewhere else did not raise any alarm from Timbo's wife and kids. The concern was mainly the unequivocal development of their home at the earliest possible time they could make. Thus they both saw the opportunity as a fast track option to achieve their dreams.

Timbo had not driven this far from home yet since settling in and thus had to study the road directory to get there. It was cold when he left and the ground fog was heavy enough to cover the road. He had to follow the tail lights of cars ahead of him. It was like driving a *James Bond car* in the sea of cloud with an eye on the road signage for his direction.

Upon arrival on site at 10.00p.m., he was at a loss when he was shown an empty room to work in. *'How am I going to work in this empty room?'* he asked the company liaison officer.

'That's what we are waiting for. You tell us what you need be done to the room and we'll fix it accordingly. We don't know your job and we don't know what's to be done', the supervisor responded courteously.

'I thought there were people working with you already?', he insinuated remembering his boss' comment on their boys going on holiday.

'That's true but not on this site. This is a new one as you can see', explained the supervisor.

'I see', Timbo finally acquiesced. *'Ok, give me a minute so I can draft something'*, he requested.

Timbo was caught off hand. He was not warned of such a situation and he did not have any drawn plans for such working environments with him. He had accepted his boss' request initially assuming everything was organised upon arrival. But he was on site then, he therefore had no choice but to draw the plan out of his wit in order to prove to the supervisor and company his potential in coming this far.

Thus, he did not only apply his educated knowledge, but also his years of experience to plan the room out. Everything was drafted free hand though the measurements were based on the equipment he had been using in the other place. The supervisor was surprised when Timbo presented him with the draft within such a short time, *'This is what's needed. Give me a call when you are ready or in doubt',* he told the supervisor.

'Good. We'll get the boys to do it by tomorrow but I'll drop you off at the hotel so you can have some rest. You've had a long drive', conceded the supervisor.

When he was called back at 6.00a.m., he was flabbergasted with the new outlook he was shown. It was beyond his expectations; it was exactly the picture he had in mind. After testing every piece of equipment, he eventually declared everything safe for them all and hence the start of the project.

After the first day, he was not sure whether or not he was really needed because he was never called to work. He just stayed put in the hotel room most of the time awaiting a call from them; there were no mobile phones then to facilitate the communications.

The first call came 4.00a.m., on the following day when the workers were having a break. He was told he would only be called during their breaks and he had to finish before resuming again. Thus, he had to be extra fast in executing his job and he had to disclose his findings before the end of the breaks so that they could rectify any problem before proceeding.

Timbo knew he could be very popular with the company for letting the work flow without hiccups or very unpopular with knocking back anything inconsistent with the institutional guidelines. Despite sympathising with the workers in the effort they put into their work, it did not waver Timbo's diligence one way or the other. It was his motto to stick with the Australian boomerang culture *'it goes and comes back'.* It would always fall back on him if any unforeseen disaster hit the project in the long run of the company.

Timbo thought this contract was a luxury. He would only work two or three hours a day at the most and enjoyed the rest of it. He did not mind it as long as the money would be paid in full when the subcontract expired. And it did.

Upon arriving back at his workplace, he was told his contract money was already paid into his account. At home that night, Timbo and his family did not only have dinner to celebrate being together again but also for the money that would take them to their new house sooner rather than later. The kids were happy and so were Timbo and his wife. That was industrial radiography.

The Spooky Bike

When Timbo was not working on a weekend, he would always pack up and go with his wife and kids to work on their newly built house half an hour away from where they were. He made an agreement with the builder to build it only but leave the painting and interior decorations to him. Luckily, he had a Russian workmate who was a professional painter previously; he kindly mentored Timbo and advised him on the type of paint to buy. His advice was helpful so that Timbo knew what would bypass an undercoat and what quantity were required for each room and the whole exterior of the house. It saved them a lot in paint and money.

One evening while painting the exterior of the house, the wind whipped strongly around them. Timbo was concentrating on the lower planks when all of a sudden the ladder he used to paint the window top was blown against the window and crushed it.

'*Oh shit. What does this mean? Things are broken when we have not even used it*', he stated drearily. He looked at his wife with a gloomy face as if resorting for support.

'*That's a call to stop. The kids are crying and need feeding too There's always another day*', she reminded him.

'*I think so too. I'll get some food for us but we'll inform the builder on Monday*', he agreed.

On the following week, he told the builder exactly what happened.

'*Don't worry my friend, I'll put it down as a result of vandalism so it does not cost you any more*', assured the builder.

Timbo hired a mini excavator for landscaping in the following weekend. He had not driven one before but the hirer showed him how. Everything went smoothly in the beginning until the machine climbed a hump. It was on the verge of rolling onto one side. Timbo reflexively stretched out his foot to stop the machine but he was quick to pull his foot back and applied the backhoe to save him. Timbo's wife screamed out loud for his safety; she was shaking in fear of the unlikely consequences. Again she called a stop to their work before anything worse would happen.

While at work one day, his wife called him to come home straightaway. *'Why? What's wrong?'* he asked.

'Builders next door excavated their land including your newly grown hedge', she answered disappointingly.

'Ok I'll see you shortly'.

Timbo excused himself from work and rushed home. She was right. All his effort in the last couple of weeks had all been scattered. He did not hesitate but confronted them assertively. They only apologised and declared they were just following instructions from their head office.

Timbo lodged a compensation claim and was finally awarded compensation after many hurdles to overcome.

Painting and landscaping were just one part of their new home dream, having a garage was another desire. Again he asked the builder to build the garage only and leave the floor concreting to him. During then, he was on contract for the pipe company that concreted the inside wall of the pipes. When he asked the manager for the cost of bags of cement for his personal use, *'They're free',* he answered.

'I'm not joking', Timbo reaffirmed.

I'm not joking too. Why are you asking?', confirmed the manager.

'I want some bags for my garage foundation. That's why I'm asking'.

'Ok come and see me after hours', stated the manager. That was another kind-heartedness gesture he could not forget. He only paid a small amount for them. By the end of the week he had enough for his garage so Timbo hired a concrete mixer and a trailer to fetch road metal.

Over the next few weekends, Timbo and his very young kids would mix the concrete while his wife and his sister who was visiting laid it out. It took them the whole day to complete the whole floor area.

On the following Saturday while working on their BBQ area in between the garage and the house, the kids came running from the garage and clung onto him.

'What's the matter? What happened?' he queried.

'The bike, our tricycle', his eldest daughter was trying to say.

'Yeah! What about it?'

'It moved around in the garage on its own'.

'It could be the wind', he tried to distract them.

'No dad. Come here', she held Timbo's hand and led him to the garage. *'Look, it was here at the door but it's now facing us from the far corner. It moved around as if someone was riding it'.*

Before anyone said anything more, surprisingly, the bike came straight to Timbo. He was not at all scared but was furious at what he saw. He just picked up the bike and threw it against the fence. He followed it up and smashed it against the driveway.

'Dad, you're wrecking our bike', cried his daughter.

'I know dear', Timbo agreed as he dumped it in the bin.

He did not want to convince them the bike was a spooky one.

He took them into the house, had a quick lunch and then took them for shopping. *'We'll buy you a new one',* he said to distract them from whatever thoughts they had.

This happened a fortnight after one of his in-laws passed away.

When the kids were in beds that night, their mother raised the issue with Timbo if there were any relationships with the ladder smashing the window, the near tilt of the excavator in the past, and the kids' spooky bike.

Timbo flatly refused to accept such view. *'If you think like that we'll never enjoy our new house',* he told his wife. *'We'll continue clearing and burn every bits and pieces of garbage lying around especially any types of bones, be them fish bones, chicken bones or whatever'.*

'What about getting the priest to bless the land and the house?' she advised.

'We'll do our bit first; if it doesn't work, then we'll get him', he insisted.

Since then nothing suspicious flickered again.

The Oil Refinery

As Timbo gained confidence in his new skill as an industrial radiographer, his reputation and popularity were also gaining momentum not only within his workplace but also amongst their clients. He was getting positive feedback from customers he worked with via his boss. Thus when the only refinery company in New Zealand rang up his boss for someone to give a third opinion on their suspended job, he was keen to send Timbo again. Before he hung up he asked Timbo to talk directly to the client so he would be aware of their expectation.

'Hello, this is Timbo speaking', he introduced himself.

'Hello Timbo, this is Terry from the Refinery Consortium. I've just been talking to your boss about our project which is now suspended because of the questionable pipe qualities. We've had two inspectors already and they've condemned the stock; we need a third opinion before returning the stock and expect a new load to continue the project. We desperately need your service because we are losing millions per day', he explained.

Timbo tried to get as much technical information on the galvanised pipes as he could from the client to prepare him on what to look for when he got there. After hanging up, Timbo disappeared into their workplace library searching for some information relevant to the problem he had been called for. He had to look hard and faster because it was near knock off time and he had to leave early the following morning.

After sifting through some textbooks, he eventually came across a half page article describing the pipes in exactly the same way the client described it on the telephone. Reading further down the page, he found out that pipes were manufactured as described to facilitate the grinding and welding. From such statement, Timbo noted there was nothing wrong with the pipes. He was happy he found the solution that grounded the project before he travelled.

There was no time to waste when he arrived on site. He went straight to work as expected. The Consortium was anxious to hear his verdict – if it would be a lifesaving or 'induced coma' to them. After an hours work the operational manager came back to him and asked, *'Well, what do you think?'.*

Timbo took a break from his work and bravely addressed the client, *'I do not think there is anything wrong with the pipes'.*

The operational manager stared at Timbo in disbelief, *'What, are you serious? We've had two inspectors already condemning the pipes and now you are saying there's nothing wrong?'.*

'Yes, I think it's just the way the pipes were manufactured to facilitate grinding and welding', Timbo confidently remarked according to the textbook information he had acquired before he left.

'Are you sure?'.

'I'm positive', confirmed Timbo.

'In that case we want you to write a report so we can fax to our London office for reassessment of the situation. They've already organised a shipment of new pipes to be delivered to us as soon as they get a third confirmation. We've also arranged shipment of pipes to be returned. But if yours is approved, we'll resume work immediately. That will save us a fortune', the operational manager declared enthusiastically.

Timbo dropped everything and followed the operational manager to the office for his report. It did not take long for him to write it; he quoted all that he saw in the pipes since arrival and justified it with the background information he absorbed before he left his main workplace. Once completed and signed, the operational manager headed straight for the Fax machine while Timbo resumed working on the pipes after his cup of tea.

It was not long when he heard the worksite siren singing loud and clear. The operational manager came out smiling and headed straight at him, *'Congratulations',* he hailed as he shook Timbo's dirty hand. *'London has accepted your report. All shipments cancelled and the project resumed as you've just heard the compound siren. You've saved us millions of dollars. That's excellent'.*

'*Thank you*', Timbo humbly replied. '*It's good to know it was worth my coming this far'.*

'*More than we expected*', complimented the operational manager. '*The management team and the workers are all happy with the result and they want you to stay for the rest of the week if that's ok with you*', he added.

'*I don't mind*', he answered with more confidence then.

'*That's good. We have organised lunch for you every day with the canteen and a hotel for your stay. Is there anything else we can help you with?*', the operational manager offered.

'*No thanks'.*

'*Ok I'll leave you to your work but feel free to give me a tinkle if need be. Thanks again for saving us*', he appreciated Timbo's service.

Timbo stayed for few more days to ascertain continuity of the work before returning home. When he was about leaving, the operational manager came back to him not only to acknowledge his service but also asked, '*Can you come back next week, Timbo?*'.

'*Sorry, no*', Timbo answered flatly.

'*Why?*'.

'*I have a wife and two young kids to look after at home?*', Timbo was not scared to reveal his domestic concern.

'*Can you bring them over?*',

'*If you pay for them up here, I can*', Timbo tentatively offered.

'*That's no problem. Bring them over; we will book them in while you do your work. How's that?*'.

'*Deal*', he smiled as they shook hands to leave.

After working the following week, Timbo decided to take the whole family for sightseeing up north to the very end of the island when they were close to it. '*We may as well go up to see the northernmost tip of the island while we are here*', he told his wife and kids.

'*Why not, this may be the only time we'll come up here*', supported his wife.

Half way up their destination, they came across some celebrations, '*Daddy, whats this?*', his kids asked.

'*I don't know dear. Let me scan the area if I can see some inkling of the incidence*', he answered. As soon as he saw the **'*Welcome to Waitangi*'** sign he quickly turned to the kids and verify the initial question, '*It must be the Waitangi Day*'[5]

'*Whats that?*', they enquired.

It's the day the Maoris handed over their land to the British to look after', he tried to explain.

'*Why are they protesting?*', insisted the eldest of the girls.

'*They probably are not getting what they initially wanted*', Timbo tried to justify the protests within celebrations. '*We'll stop here for lunch and witness the occasion because we may never have another time to come again this far before we go home*'.

By the time they returned home no one could explain the role of their protests during the celebrations. Timbo could not be bothered asking. They just enjoyed their lunch and watched. There was a group of entertainers performing some traditional war dances, *the Haka,* to entertain visitors; there was also a different group chanting some rhymes of protest to the official team.

Before leaving they went for a quick tour of the place especially the building where the *'treaty'* was signed. Timbo and family were very impressed with the care accorded to the building and contents; they were all in immaculate conditions. They bought a copy of the deed as a souvenir for their unplanned visit and signed the visitors' book. *It looks like none of our clan came this far according to the book*', Timbo commented after flicking through a few used pages of the book.

---

5   *Treaty of Waitangi, 1840*

'It's either that or they are not interested', added his wife as they made for the car. *'Do you still insist on going to the northern most tip of the island?'*, she checked with Timbo.

'I don't think so. It's getting late for us if we are to go home today. What do you think?', he confirmed with her.

'I agree. That's why I'm asking. The kids are starting to wear out. It's a fair way back home and you are the only driver', she advocated.

'Good, let's go home then', he surrendered.

It was dark but the night was still young when they arrived home safely. They were all tired but joyful of the opportunity they had for a brief break from home.

'Well, that was nice of them to pay for our short get away', cheered the wife after putting their children in bed. .

'Yep, that's industrial radiography', joked Timbo.

Change of Heart

He was more than grateful with this job because it gave him the chance to see most of the places like the one they had just been with the wife and children. Moreover, they were also given a car to use after hours and the weekend when he's free, a privilege he would never get if he was working as a medical radiographer. He was therefore of the thought he would stick with it for as long as everything is in harmony with his family. The only hiccup was the late finish and frequent time away from home and the short trips to the outskirt of the country.

In one of his trips, he was threatened on the road by some unknown travellers. It was a fair distance from home and he had to speed up a bit to get home before his children would go to sleep.

It was dark in the middle of nowhere when he overtook this car with three guys in it. He was not aware such a move upset them until they overtook him again. Their car almost swiped his car if he had not swerved away. He started to sense trouble when they slowed down after they overtook him. His thoughts were with the wife and children whatever the consequences of this seemingly road race would be. He wanted to overtake again and sped away from them but was not confident of his car capacity. It might not be powerful enough to surpass theirs, or they might catch up with him again and that could be disastrous if not fatal for him.

Moreover, these guys could be locals and they would have some friends they could call to barricade the road ahead of him and that could be his fate. Thus, he had to keep a distance from them in the rear and try not to annoy them more. When they stopped at the gas station, he felt very relieved. He kept going in the same speed when he passed them but once they were out of sight, he pressed hard down on the accelerator and sped away hoping they would not follow him again.

After a while he saw in his rear mirror car lights slowly getting brighter indicative of a speeding one following him. He had to hit the floor hard with the accelerator if he had to keep a distance from them. He knew if he be stopped by the cops on the road for speeding, it would be a safety net for him from his followers despite being penalised for speeding. But to his relief he reached the main highway without being caught by police radar or his chasers'.

When he got home, the children were already asleep but the wife met him at the door, *'I was scared when you were late'*, she admitted.

'Me too, I was more than scared I may not make it home', he responded.

'Why?'

'These stupid guys were blocking my way but I was lucky they ran out of gas. As soon as they stopped at the gas station I pressed hard on the pedal and only slowed down when some oncoming driver would flash their lights to warn us of mobile police radar ahead. But I'm here now, that's the main thing', he cheered her up.

'What about you, are you ok?'

'Of course I'm always fine when the whole family is'.

'What about the kids?'

'They wanted to stay awake for your arrival but they could not make it', she recounted.

Timbo had to start early for the next job the following day. He would leave them again before they wake up and he was not so sure if he would finish early or late again.

Timbo realised the pain of not seeing his children before or after hours due to his long working hours. Despite all the perks he had been given as an industrial radiographer like the company car and several allowances, he still felt he was missing something very important in his life, the company of his children.

His children were feeling the same as well. He understood that he would be drummed to it someday but he was not quite sure when. Thus, when he called on them to kiss goodbye before he left for another outskirt job, his eldest daughter refused but cried, 'Oh no, you just come and go but you never want to stay with us'.

Timbo heard her and it really hit him hard. When he went over to hug her she ran away from him and it hurt him even more. When he finally caught up with her, 'I'm sorry if I hurt you for being away but I have to get the money to feed us', he tried to console her. 'But I promise not to in the near future, ok?', he assured her. She just sobbed and nodded but did not say a word. Timbo on the other hand hugged her closer as an assuring gesture before he left.

Timbo was in a different mood altogether. Her cry warned him to rethink his priority, the money or his family. Although he was comfortable with the current job, he thought he was still a medical radiographer, an option that could satisfy them all when an opportunity arose. Thus, when he saw the vacancy in the paper, he had no hesitation but called for it.

When told he got it, he thought this couldn't have come at any other time; whether it was mere coincidence or a divine response to his daughter's cry, only God knew. But he accepted it as an answer to his uneasiness over his job comfort and his family's discomfort.

When he saw his boss the following morning, 'Can I see you for a minute?' he asked him.

'Sure, come inside', the boss accepted as he opened the door for him. 'Yes, what can I do for you?', the boss asked unsuspectingly.

'I'm sorry but I'm leaving', he declared unconditionally.

'Oh no, this can't be true. Are you serious Timbo? What have we done wrong? If I offer you another pay rise will it change your plan?', the boss responded possessively. It was obvious he did not want Timbo to leave.

'No sir, there is nothing wrong in the company. Money is not the problem too. I'm very happy to continue but it's for the sake of my family. I was not aware of their feelings until last week when one of my daughters refused to say goodbye before I left. She said I was only coming and going but never wanted to stay with them. That's why I'm leaving. I'm sorry to say that but it is for their sake that I have to. I'm very happy with you and everyone in the company', he tried to convince the boss.

'I see. That's understandable and I am sorry if we have been keeping you away from your family too often', he accepted the resignation apologetically. 'So is there another job lined up for you?', he asked.

'Yes, I'm going back to my original field, the medical one in the hospital'

'That's good. As long as you have a job to feed the family I'm happy too. So when are you leaving?', he tried to confirm.

'In two weeks.'

'Have you got a car yet?', the boss asked.

'I'll try and get one before I start in the next job', Timbo openly declared.

'Well, when you leave, take the car you're using to start with and return it when you get one. Thank you for letting me know and many thanks indeed for your service. We'll sorely miss you. Don't forget, the door is still opened for you whenever you want to come back or when things don't work out the other side', he offered appreciatively.

'Thank you very much for your kind consideration. Many thanks for the opportunity to work with you. It was a very challenging one', he finally had the chance to acknowledge his employer.

Though he had only a couple of weeks left with this company, he felt as if he had just started with them. The feeling that he would fulfil his promise to his daughter and his unconditional welcome back to the company were other win-win indications of their journey. They would still continue as usual in a changed working environment without alienating anyone.

The wife and children were vivaciously joyful. *'I can sleep soundly now the next time you are late; I do not have to worry anymore on whether or not you will ever be home because I can always call the hospital to check on you',* his wife joked.

'Don't forget I can always go back to my old job if you keep hassling me in the new one', he countered humorously.

Career Highlights

An old lady from his home country was admitted in the Emergency department for severe abdominal pain. Her clinical findings indicated suspected food poisoning. Thus, she was brought into the X-rays department for a special x-ray examination of her bowel. She could not speak a language other than her own. The communication problem hindered the start of the examination. The pain was so excruciating that she could barely speak but moaning as she rolled into a ball.

Timbo was working on that day but in a different section of the department. He was taken by surprise when a nurse came over to him, *'Excuse me Timbo, your help is needed over in our section',* begged the nurse.

'What's the problem?' queried Timbo.

'There's an old lady in great agony but she can't speak or understand English. She looks like she doesn't want the examination done', explained the nurse. *'She is one of your clans but she is on her own. You may be able to talk to her in your language'.*

'Sure. I can try', he offered.

Timbo did not hesitate but followed the nurse to the old lady. When he got there, she was jumping all over the bed to get some relief from the pain. When he leaned over the bed trying to talk and calm her down, she reached for his hand and begged not to have an X-ray. Despite Timbo's effort to explain the benefits of having one so that doctors could diagnose and treat her correctly, it made her sob even more. She wasn't just crying, she was reeling from side to side, and thumbing the hospital bed to release the pain. Despite the agony, she adamantly refused the examination.

When Timbo felt beyond doubt that she could not be persuaded, he eventually surrendered. He convinced the team not to proceed in case something might happen against her will.

'I'm sorry guys, I can't help you', he apologised the team.

'That's fine. You've tried your best. We'll send her back to the Emergency and I'll speak to the requesting doctor. Thanks for the effort', commended the radiologist.

The lady's crying started to subside. She was very grateful to Timbo for accepting her wish. Timbo was not quite sure whether her hysteria was genuine or aggravated because of fear of the examination. Nonetheless, he did all he could do to help her understand the procedure doctors thought necessary to reach a diagnosis and hence the appropriate treatment.

The following weekend he worked alone from midnight till 8.00a.m. on both the Friday and Saturday nights. Both nights weren't so easy. They were nights where many, especially the working class, would celebrate their weeks work. Timbo never looked forward to such shifts but he had to abide by the roster like his colleagues.

After 2.00 o'clock on Saturday morning, the nurse in charge of the emergency unit sneaked into the X-rays department and warned Timbo of his next patient. *'Your next patient is heavily intoxicated and is with his mates who also smell alcohol. They had a brawl somewhere in town and one of theirs was fatally injured, and that's why they are very violent and refuse to listen to anyone. Be very careful when they come. Call security if you feel threatened. Good luck'*, she warned before she left.

'Thanks', responded Timbo.

It was not long after the nurse left when the buzzer went off for the door to be opened. To Timbo's expectation, this was the patient he was warned for. The charge nurse was correct; it was the intoxicated patient and his clan. When he was brought into the X-ray room, his mates also entered and physically filled the room.

Timbo felt a chill speeding up his spine but tried his best to keep his cool. It was the first time he had to deal with such a situation. They were not only drunk but massive in body build. He had to keep his distance and be diplomatic. As soon as he saw the patient getting violent and tried to grab the X-ray machine cables, he braved himself and politely told the patient, '*Look here sir, those cables are high voltage ones. Once they snap, we'll all be gone, and you'll be the first to go, and that's why you should not attempt anything unfavourable*', he warned. He turned to his mates, '*That's why its safe if you stay out of the room if you don't mind*'.

He took advantage of such actions to talk them out of the room. And they listened. They slowly filed out of the room until he was left with the patient only. When the X-ray examination was done, he was shocked to be acknowledged by the patient for his service. So were his mates. He too returned the gratitude for respecting his word. He could not believe the success of his trick that led to the feasibility of the study.

When the charge nurse returned later in the night, she was impressed with the way he handled them.

'*What did you do to them mate?*' she wondered. '*They came back completely different people compared to the time they first arrived*'.

'*Oh you know, I did it the island way. I just stood my ground and told them off*', he laughed and scoffed at her concern without declaring his own fear. After joking, '*I did the best diplomacy of my life and explained the fatal consequences of fiddling with high voltage X-ray cables, and they listened. That's why they cooperated and voluntarily removed themselves from the room*', he explained.

'*Well done mate. Good on you. I'm very impressed*', she laughed as she returned to her work station.

When his colleague asked him if he could do her shift the following Saturday, he was not looking forward to it because of his previous experience. However, he still agreed to it out of respect.

During the day, he was busy running around doing last minute shopping for his mother's trip back home in the evening flight. When he started working again, he prayed dutifully to be busy the whole night in case he might fall asleep because of the day's unrest. His prayer was answered in the first two hours. But as soon as he took the seat when there was break around 3.00a.m, that's when he unconsciously knocked off. When he woke up, it was already 6.00 in the morning. The same nurse that warned him before in the previous weekend came around and asked, *'Hey Timbo, are you alright? What happened?'*

'Why, what's wrong?' he wondered.

'We've been paging, we've been calling through the intercom and the phone kept ringing but no one answered. What's the trouble?'. she inquired.

'Are you sure?', he tried to confirm.

'Yeah. I was worried', she assured him.

'Oh my God, I'm very sorry. I was very busy the whole day yesterday and was hoping for a constant workload to keep me awake but I just did not know the time I knocked off', he tried to explain. The nurse just laughed and teased him.

'So where are the patients?' he asked.

'We kept them all in the rooms'.

'Has anyone complained yet?' he questioned

'No. I just told them you are busy', she assured him

'Oh! How nice of you! Can you start sending them over now before the next shift of the staff arrive'.

She laughed as she left, *'No problem, I'll start sending them now'.*

'Thanks again', he called her as she disappeared.

The workload was all cleared before the next shift worker arrived at 8.00o'clock. During the following week he was still in a panic if his boss would call him because of such professional discrepancy. But he never was.

When he met the same nurse again in the staff cafeteria, he could not get over her due consideration in saving him from such unlikelihood. She was only laughing and teased him and commented, *'Team work mate, the island way'.*

'That's very true. Team work alright', he confirmed appreciatively.

That was clinical experience.

The Eleven Year Old Boy

The day was busy in the X-ray department and Timbo was busy too. He was not aware of the types of patients coming and going. However when he called one patient, he noted he had bilateral prosthetic lower legs. He was active and responsive like any other normal person. He was with his mother.

To Timbo, they were just like any other patient. Thus, he introduced himself to them as they walked into the X-ray room. After confirming the patient's identity, the mother asked, '*Excuse me, have you been working here more than ten years?*'

'*Yes, more than that*', Timbo confirmed while uploading the patient's name onto the system. He was not aware of what the mother was getting at until she said, '*You did his first X-ray when he was six months old*'.

'*Oh, so I can't be naughty*', he jokingly responded. The mother just gave a receptive smile but did not comment.

While doing her son's X-ray, he was trying to rewind his mental computer if he could recall the appearance of this child eleven years past. By the end of the examination, he had managed to recall this child on his first presentation. He remembered clearly his parents and the baby wrapped in his blanket in the push chair as if it was the day before.

As soon as he asked the parents to take the blanket off and bring him up onto the examination table, the mother could not control her emotions but burst into tears. Timbo was shocked because he did not know why she cried until after the blanket was taken off. To his surprise, the child did not have any lower limbs. Thus, when they sat him on the table he wriggled forward enthusiastically to his parents. That aggravated his mother's cry harder. The father was cheering him on at first until he too could not contain his emotions anymore and joined his wife.

'*Don't worry. He's alright. He is a lot better than some other kids we've had*', Timbo tried to comfort them. He was emotional too but he knew he had to be strong for the parents. It was only after they calmed down that Timbo started doing the X-ray. After the examination, they seemed more relaxed though the mother was still in tears and could not say a word.

Eleven years on, Timbo was amazed at how technology changed this boy's life, let alone the parents' attitude. The mother must have been happy to see Timbo again. After the examination, she fully commended Timbo for his approach when they first came eleven years ago, '*That was why I asked earlier for the length of time you were here. I just wanted to make sure. My husband and I did not have time to say thank you after our first visit*', she justified. '*We were and are very grateful for your due understanding and support during our down time*', she continued. '*Many thanks for the job well done*', she said in farewell as they left the room.

Timbo was not prepared for such a moment. He only managed to say, '*You're welcomed*'. He could not believe someone would come back after eleven years to thank him for his service. It really made his day. He reckoned he got more satisfaction from this compliment than receiving his pay on the same week. It became an incentive for him to continue working. He was really overwhelmed with such compliment.

Running for life

During Timbo's training he did not have enough time to observe all examinations. This was mainly due to tight schedule in lectures and the practical training roster. He was not the only student in training; there were others too who were in the same situation He realised that he had to attend some weekend sessions, if there were any, to observe some of the examinations he had not seen.

Timbo was told there would be emergency cases over the weekend. He was welcomed to attend and observe if he was free. Timbo was happy to attend.

The day started with the special X-ray examination for the patient's heart blood supply. It was Timbo's first time as a student to observe and assist the X-ray team inside the operating suite. His supervisor briefed Timbo on the reason for the examination and his role when asked during the examination.

Timbo did not know there was something wrong with the procedure until someone called to press the emergency button. There was sudden unrest in the room. The emergency team arrived and performed their revival skill but it was late. No one said anything. Staff appeared shocked and depressed. Timbo did not inquire, as a student, what the problem was and its cause. He just followed his supervisor to the tearoom and waited for the next call to action.

It was only after their tea break that Timbo's supervisor revealed the cause of the first patient's malady to be due to cardiac arrest. Timbo's mind was finally relaxed but sad because it was his first to observe but turned out to be fatal, if not traumatic.

There were two more patients in their beds lining up the passage to the suite for a similar examination. As soon as the second one heard that his predecessor passed away during the procedure, he quickly got up and left. Timbo's team was surprised to find no one outside when they came for him.

Timbo was not impressed and so was his supervisor.

'*I would have done the same if I was him too*', joked Timbo's supervisor as they prepared for the next patient.

It was Timbo's first exposure to such a situation. From it, he learnt to be alert at all times, and to be calm and professional before, during and after the execution of the procedure. He also learnt that besides acquiring professional skill, he had to realise that, despite the team's best effort to achieve the best possible outcome, life would not always turn out positively. There would also be some unforeseen circumstances that hindered success sometimes.

The Unwanted Old Sod

During the week, an old patient was brought to the department in a wheelchair in the company of a nurse. He was for a chest X-ray. He was still mobile but very slow. He was in a hospital gown and a white pyjama.

'*G'day sir*', greeted Timbo in his newly acquired Aussie slang. '*I'm Timbo. I'll be doing your X-ray. How about you, what is your name?*

'*Hi, I'm Harry. Harry Carter*'.

'*Do you know the type of X-ray you are here for?*'

'*I was admitted in hospital for my tummy but I'm here for a chest X-ray. I don't know why. Do you mind checking if they are ordering the right thing?*' he asked Timbo.

'*No, not at all, just give me a second*', he assured the patient. Timbo thought it would be fast but it took him a few phone calls to make before he finally reached the medical officer who ordered the examination '*Hello, it's Dr Skiffy speaking*',

'*Hello Dr Skiffy, this is Timbo, the radiographer from the X-ray Department*', he introduced himself.

'*Yes?*'

'*I have Mr Carter, Harry Carter, a patient of yours with me for an X-ray of his chest as you ordered. He was admitted for abdominal problem. But he is querying the appropriateness of the examination despite my endeavour to convince him that it was consistent with the clinical notes you wrote on the form*', he explained.

'*Sorry, but there's million patients seen and I cannot recall all of them instantly*', Dr Skiffy responded in a more light hearted mood.

'*That's very true, it's understandable*', added Timbo.

'*Can I have his Medical Record Number please?*'

'*Sure.*'

Timbo could hear over the phone Dr Skiffy punching the numbers on his keyboard as he read them out. In a matter of seconds, '*Oh yes*', he responded. '*He is for an operation tomorrow; it's a pre-operative check. Please do the examination and tell him I will see him in his room after lunch*'.

'*Many thanks.*'

'*My pleasure*', concluded Dr Skiffy

By the time Timbo got back to Mr Carter, he was getting impatient, '*Where the hell have you been?*' he blasted Timbo. '*I've been left in this room like an unwanted old sod while you take your time yarning here and there. Is this the kind of service you provide?*

'*I'm sorry sir, but it took a number of phone calls before I got hold of Dr Skiffy who ordered your X-ray*', Timbo apologised as he tried to justify his actions.

'This is terribly unacceptable', Mr Carter continued. Timbo kept trying to pacify him but his voice got louder and louder until it attracted the boss' attention. When the boss poked his nose for a quick peek, he was stunned to see Mr Carter, an old friend from high school, *'Hey, what are you doing here?'* the boss greeted him socially.

Mr Carter, in a change of mood, chuckled in return and joked, *'Looking for a schooner, what else'*. The boss bursted out laughing knowing Mr Carter's character, he was referring to a big glass of beer as they used to share after their golfing when free.

While chatting humorously, Timbo thought that could be the cause of Mr Carter's hysteria – him thinking he should be treated like a friend of the boss instead of an old bag. He was otherwise thankful to his boss for diffusing Mr Carter's electrical madness.

Before the boss left, he told Mr Carter in a soothing tone, *'Have your X-ray done and I'll have a look at it'*. Timbo did not have to justify the Dr's order again as initially done but proceeded with the X-ray.

Mr Carter's tummy bulged out of norm as if he was carrying a term baby. When demonstrating his breathing technique, Timbo noted that Mr Carter's tummy melted inward when he breathed in. Thus, when asked to breathe for his X-ray, his pants got loose and dropped unexpectedly. Just before Timbo pressed the button for the X-ray, Mr Carter let go of his machine grip and tried speedily to reach for his pants. Unfortunately, his reflex was not that fast enough. Before he reached for it, his pant was already down his ankles. *'Oh my...'*, he exclaimed as he bent down for his pants.

To Timbo's disbelief, Mr Carter did not have any undie and he was really exposed. Instead of reacting immaturely, he ran up and helped Mr Carter with his pants and hence his posture again. But the nurse accompanying him could not contain her emotions. She just hid behind the machine and quietly laughed hysterically to avoid causing Mr Carter any embarrassment. She thought it was hilarious.

'I'm sorry mate', Mr Carter apologised.

'Don't worry sir. It's ok. You're not the first one. We'll try again if that's ok', comforted Timbo.

'*Thanks*', reacted Mr Carter.

After the X-ray, Mr Carter thanked Timbo again and apologised for his madness earlier. Timbo diplomatically returned the compliment and also apologised for keeping him waiting.

The nurse, on the other hand, gave Timbo a cheeky wink because of her patient's 'publicity stunt' as she wheeled him out of the room. That was a clinical experience. It was an experience that did not only challenge his wit but also his professional conscience.

Looking Yonder

5th Door: The Saudi Call

Timbo had heard of jobs in the Middle Eastern countries like Saudi Arabia and Dubai, just to mention a few but did not know the entrance criteria into them. He had no intention of leaving his family even though he was curious to look yonder. His only knowledge of the countries was through the biblical accounts but that was ages ago. He thought it would be worth a visit to see some of the landmarks quoted in the Christian bible.

When he came across an advertisement in the paper for radiographers' positions in the Saudis he decided to give it a try. After supplying all the required documentations including results of medical tests, he was eventually offered a post in one of the hospitals. Everything would be paid for like airfares, accommodation and salary. It was an opening he never dreamt to be in sight had he continued working as an industrial radiographer. It was too good to ignore.

However, he had relinquished his previous job because of family. He was then faced with a big challenge whether or not to take the offer. Timbo decided to forego it and concentrated on their current circumstances. They were still comfortable with it and there was no need to look yonder.

His wife was aware of the opportunity too. When she did not hear about it from him after a while, she questioned Timbo for it, *'What's happening to the job offer from Saudi Arabia?'*

'It's still opened', he answered discreetly.

'Are you not taking it?' she queried curiously.

'I don''t think so'.

'Why?', she persistently asked.

'I feel for you and the kids especially the promise I made to my daughter', he tried to rationalize his actions.

'I think you should take it. It's not very often people get such an opportunity. Don't worry about me and the kids, we'll manage alright. I'm sure the kids will be proud too of your blessing if explained properly to them. You should take the chance; you can only get it once', she encouraged.

'I'll give it another thought if that's what you think', he answered respectfully.

Timbo was shocked at his wife's advice. She was very brave in offering to fend for her and the kids so he could assume the post.

When the Recruitment agent contacted him again on the finalization of his appointment he ultimately responded with his wife's blessing.

The Sunset that Never Set

Timbo had been taught from a young age that the world is round. But, every now and then, when he listened to some speeches, they referred to the world as having four corners; it made him think twice whether the world was really round or flat. These were the two elements that had been baffling him till then. He could not fully resist or embrace either of them but just went with the flow.

The fourteen hour flight he took to Saudi Arabia was the longest he had ever been. It was the most exciting one too because of travelling with people with different cultures and languages. The captain kept updating them on the countries they were flying over. Each time he did so, Timbo would peek outside to have a glimpse of each country's landscape. It was then that the sun's approach to the horizon caught his attention. Each time he would peek outside, the sun was approaching the horizon.

When he looked out the next time expecting darkness, the sun was a bit further away from the horizon. He kept doing it to check when the sun would set. Amazingly it never did by the time the plane landed. *'Does this mean the world is round? It should have set already if it was flat'*, he asked himself. He was grateful that he had seen it himself; if anyone told him the sun never set during the whole time of his flight he would never believe it.

One thing he strongly admired while on the plane was the praying space at the back of the airline he was travelling in. He was getting stiff after sitting for quite a while, and he decided to take a stride to the back of the plane. In most airplanes, the kitchen or the stewards' working area cover the area behind the last seats. To his amazement, this plane had an isle continuing past the airline kitchen. He kept sticking his nose past the kitchen in curiosity. To his surprise, he could see people praying. It was the first time for him to eyewitness a plane space allocated especially for praying.

'Wow! This is cool. Why isn't this allocated in all planes?', he wondered. *'They really need them for divine guidance'*, he kept rousing himself as he returned to his seat.

The announcement to prepare for landing came half an hour before arrival. When he checked again on the sun, it was halfway down the horizon. The glitter of the country lights started to take over. It was just as colorful as glowing stars lighting the path to welcome new arrivals like him. In his way of thinking they were undoubtedly travelling with the 'Sun'[6]

Upon landing he hailed it with great awe. The weather was identical to his home country and he liked it. Timbo had no idea who was coming to meet him at the airport. As he exited the customs clearance area, he saw a long line of locals holding placards with names on them. He was relieved when he saw his last name displayed there also.

Timbo walked straight to him and the driver gave a warm welcoming gesture and took him to the car. Both of them were excited but could not communicate. Neither of them could speak the other's language. He just gave a nod to what the driver was gesturing about and hence laughed when he laughed. He felt sorry and thankful for his driver in trying to entertain their trip but he was useless linguistically. It was a conversation lost in translation.

---

6   Connotation for 'Son'.

Timbo had no knowledge of the location of the hospital he was heading for and the distance from the airport. His heartbeat only returned to normal when he saw the hospital sign on the road they were turning into. He wished he could speak the language to express his heartfelt gratitude to the driver but only held his hands tightly and shook them vibrantly to show his appreciation before he left.

He noted the tight security of the compound they were entering when they stopped and checked at the gate before proceeding to where his new boss was waiting.

'*Welcome to Saudi Arabia*', the new boss greeted Timbo with his Irish accent.

'*Thank you*', Timbo acknowledged.

'*How was your trip?*', the boss asked.

'*Very long and tiring but I'm here now*', he stated.

'*That's the main thing. I won't keep you long*'. He showed him his room and associated facilities and handed over his key after chatting over his late dinner. '*You need a good rest and I'll see you tomorrow*', he concluded before leaving.

Timbo recollected the distance and time he had travelled, he could only be grateful for his safe arrival. This was a trip from one side of the globe to the other laterally, and from one hemisphere to the other longitudinally. It reminded him of his father's response when begging to see their home town, '*If you do well in school you will not only see our home town, but you will also see the rest of the world*'. He had eventually seen the fruition of such a prediction.

Thus he could not stop thanking his parents for their support and the challenge that plodded him on. He was even more grateful for the Divine guidance and the kindness of his sponsors in continuing his parent's effort. Moreover, he could not forget his wife and children whose encouragement resulted in achieving his father's prophecy.

The night was one of the very short nights he slept. He could not wait to see the place, its landscape, vegetation and the people. Looking out from his window in the morning, the sky was clear and the flat land expanded beyond his vision. The people in the compound were all expatriates. They were all diverging to the hospital about twenty minutes walking distance. Some took the courtesy bus running continuously to and from the hospital. He followed them. He noted that almost all employees in specialised fields like his were from the northern hemisphere.

He later observed there were two compounds, the one for those in specialised fields and the other for domestic services. Timbo was grateful with his previous sponsors without whom he would not be in a specialised field that entitled him for accommodation in the former. The hospital provided each compound a courtesy shopping bus every evening after hours; the former having a big spacious one while the latter was a twenty-two seater.

His first trip to the shopping was awesome. It gave him a very good chance to scan the country's landscape. The most spectacular one was the Red Sea. The sun was sitting pretty on the horizon and was radiantly 'bloody' red in appearance; its reflections made the sea looked red. To prove it was not the water that was really red, he took time to physically scoop the Red Sea water in his own hands and convinced himself it was clear like any other sea water.

'Well, I can tell my people when I return home that I've seen and touched the Red Sea water and proven myself that its the reflections of the sun's red rays that's making the sea look red', he convinced himself as he marveled over the biblical landmarks he used to read about.

How the tribe crossed it was beyond his comprehension. He could not see the other bank or its outline. If he remembered correctly, the distance between the two main islands of his country was far shorter than between the Red Sea two banks. On a fine day back at home, he could see the mountain outline of the other island from where he was to take the ferry across. This was not the case in this Red sea; it was too wide for his eyes to see.

When Cultures Meet

Timbo had to adapt to the cultures of the expatriates he was working with and that of the locals. The latter was similar to his roots while the former was identical to that of the foster home he was first exposed to during his studies. Thank be to them for such thoughtfulness. He was therefore versatile either way excepting that he had to pick up faster on the local language to be more efficient in his job.

The locals' hospitality was phenomenal. He did not know if his working colleagues were getting the same treatment but he was very impressed with the reception he was receiving in all stores he entered. Whether or not it was his dark complex he was not sure. But he could not be any happier with their attitude; they were very receptive.

Timbo was shocked to meet a patient with the same surname as his. He forgot that his surname was biblically related and most of the biblical stories were about people in the area he was mixing with then. He did not reveal it to the patient but he just gave a welcoming smile and got on with what he was supposed to do.

Each morning, he was awoken by the prayer call from the speakers on the very top tip of the nearby mosque. His room was just at the same height as the speakers and they woke him. When he heard the prayer in local language, it reminded him of his father; this used to be the same time he would wake up to pray for them back then. Thus, he also got up and offered his prayer from his room. This was the normal practice each morning for the speakers to wake him up and hence became his routine to follow suit though in his own language and religion.

When he went shopping in the shop nearby, he was taken aback when the shopkeeper greeted him with open arms and said, *'Al humdulilah'*. He only shook his hand and gave a thank you smile but could not say a word. It was not because of his rudeness not to respond but mainly his ignorance of the local language. When he recounted the event to his local workmate on the following day and asked for the meaning, she just laughed and said, *'That's the culture in greeting guests. What he said was "God be with you"'*.

'Thanks. So you can be my language tutor', he acknowledged her assistance.

'No problem, be my guest', she accepted the request.

Timbo embraced everything he noted when he went shopping. The shops were westernized in layout and in the goods they sold. When the prayer call came through the shopping speakers, all the shops would close unconditionally.

Comparing it to his home country, he did not think the major traders would abide. There would always be some sneaky stores back home that would try to beat the system either because of their reputations or there were some tourists inside at the time of prayer. But, with what he eye witnessed, there were no exceptions, everyone had to leave the stores to be back when the next call came, regardless of whether you were a tourist or local.

One afternoon during 'Prayer time', he sat together with one of the locals on the long seat facing the Prayer house and watched silently the process. When the fast broke, Timbo was taken by surprise when this local turned to him, unwrapped his food and signaled to Timbo, '*Here*', as he pointed to the food.

'*No thanks*', Timbo politely refused

'*No, look plenty.*' The local tried to convince Timbo

'*No thanks, I'm not hungry*', Timbo tried to stand his ground.

'*No, please, it's my culture. Please take something*', the local insisted.

Timbo realised it would be very rude for him if he did not accept his neighbour's plea. The local's culture was just as important as his back home. Thus, he gratefully faced the local and shared his meal as if they knew each other before. It immediately reminded him of his people at home; they did exactly the same thing. It did not matter whether or not you knew him before; he would always be invited to share the meal when it was time for feed.

Timbo understood the mentality behind the offer and thus accepted it even for a tiny bit. The local was very happy that Timbo accepted his offer. Timbo gave the local money as a reciprocate token for the favour like what he was used to back home, but the local totally refused it. He never took anything from Timbo. Timbo felt bad but understood the local's reaction. It would have been the same reaction if this was back at home.

When the 'Prayer Time' was over and the shops re-opened, Timbo shook the local's hands in both hands and thanked him whole-heartedly for his sharing kindness. He never forgot such good gestures. He was grateful that he was accorded such favour when he was familiar with the culture like his. Had he not understood it, their companionship could end up differently.

He treasured highly the sponsorship and appreciated being given this opportunity. Without it, he would not know the similarity in his and their cultures despite the phenomenal geographical distances. He never forgot it.

Australia in the Agenda

Before Timbo took his first sponsored trip back home, he had already organised with his wife to meet up in Sydney for a holiday. After comparing cost of things, they found out Australia was cheaper overall especially with groceries. Moreover they would fit in nicely with its multicultural status.

He was confident there would be no problem for a job because he was not only Australian qualified but his years of experience ranged from a single X-ray room to a multi-storey department. Moreover, if he could not find a medical one, he would try the industrial one. Thus, he and his wife agreed it would be a good idea to move over to Australia.

'*Why?* asked Ira, the eldest daughter.

'*Australia is a land of opportunities. It is also a gateway to and from the other side of the world. Most importantly, she helped me get this far. It would be a nice gesture to give her something back as a token of appreciation*', Timbo tried to convince her.

'*What about our house?*'

'*Don't worry dear, I'm sure we'll get a better one in Sydney*', he assured her and her little sister.

'*Ohhhhh! What about my friends and uncles and aunties?*', she frowned at the idea.

'*Australia is a big country, so you will get many more friends; your uncles and aunties can come over and visit us one day*', he offered a comforting response.

'*Dad is right. We can even go back and visit them during school breaks*', added their mother.

'*Really?*', Ira seriously reaffirmed.

'*Yep, I don't see why not*', Timbo confirmed.

On the morning of Timbo's return flight to Saudi, Ira unexpectedly fell sick. She threw up in her sleep early dawn.

'*I don't think I should go now that Ira is sick*', he whispered his wife.

'*No, you should abide by the contract. She'll be alright for sure. I'll take care of her. If you break the contract, it will have a long term bad effect on your record and will hinder you any other future job consideration both locally and abroad*', his wife encouraged him.

'*Are you sure, its not a half hour or two hours flight. It will be another four days to take if anything worse warrants my return*'.

'*I know what to do but get yourself ready before it's late to the airport*', she insisted.

Timbo had every faith in his wife and therefore took her advice.

When Timbo arrived back in his Saudi workplace, he was just talking openly to his mates how much he missed his family. His boss had no hesitation but confronted him. '*There is rumour about your despair over missing your family. Is this true?*', he asked.

'*Very much so, sir*', he answered.

'*I don't want to pressure you but for the department's future staffing, do you think you will extend your contract?*', the boss tried to be diplomatic.

'*I understand, and to be honest with you, I don't think so. I'm sorry about that*', he was upfront with his answer.

'*There's no need to apologize. We do understand. Thanks for being honest and your revelation. There is still plenty of time if you do change your mind. I'll be even happier too if you stay. But do what is best for you and your family',* he confided.

'*Thanks',* Timbo expressed his appreciation.

It was always his conviction not to revert to his previous platform of service after conveying his decision. He did it before he took up radiography as an option when first approached by his home health director, he did it before he left for New Zealand, he also did it before he left for Saudis, and so was this one too. All he had to do was to organise with his wife their departure from New Zealand and plan his departure from his current employment a gradual elegant one.

Tough Start

Starting afresh in a different place was a tough one. Unlike their start in New Zealand where he looked for fully furnished abode, this one did not have anything at all. There was no fridge, no dining table. As a result they used the esky with ice as a starting fridge and the floor covered with newspaper for dining. It did not look like they were in Australia but they had to make do with what they had until they finally bought furniture and the fridge. It was his choice for his kids to eyewitness their starting point in Australia. It challenged them to strive for the best but not be pampered with everything. Thus they would appreciate life from the lowest point upward like his.

It was not hard for Timbo to get a job; each hospital accepted him when he inquired during then. The choice was his and therefore chose the one closer to home. He did not have a car then but the bus stop was in front of their house; it was not a great deal getting to and from work using public transport.

However, when he started working afternoon shifts, it was then that he realised the importance of having their own car. His shift finished midnight but the last train stopped 11.00pm and the last bus for him would be 11.30pm then. Taking a taxi after each night of the week was suicidal to him financially. Thus, he decided to hit the street. He arrived home two hours later. The wife was still awake wondering where he was and she was more than relieved to open the door when she heard his voice; there were no mobile phones then to facilitate communications.

The shift continued for five days and he had been trying all short routes to get a bit earlier but they seemed all the same. He always carried a meter long stick to fend off any wild dog after him. On the last night, he was halfway home when he felt his bag being pulled from behind. He staggered backward but managed to hold his balance. When he turned around, one guy was trying to drag his bag while another started attacking him. He reacted uninhibitedly and swung his stick around uncontrollably; he heard it hitting someone but did not know which one. He swung again forcefully and hit another one; he felt his bag released.

The two retreated and disappeared into the darkness. He must have hurt them seriously. He couldn't be bothered chasing them but continued home speedily with his bag in his front this time. He only told his wife the following morning when he stopped her from throwing his stick to the bin.

'Why, it's just a stick',

'I know but its my defending weapon; it helped me last night in warding off the thugs', he declared.

'What happened?', she showed a keen interest.

'Some guys tried to snatch my bag on the road but I whacked them off harshly with my stick and did not return'.

'You didn't say anything last night', she sounded concerned.

'I know. I didn't want to trouble you', he calmed her down.

On the weekend he went with his daughter car shopping. Again it was a long walk from one car dealer to the next until they got to one running a promotional sausage sizzle; they were grateful to be treated with such even though they did not buy a car from there. He looked at his daughter as she smashed the sausage in seconds; he applauded her for persevering the long walk. She looked back at him with a big innocent smile as she soothed it up with the cold sweet drink.

'That's nice of them', she commented joyfully.

'Yeah, it is just what we wanted, was not it?', he added.

'What next?', she prompted him.

'I think we better go back home and make an assessment of the different prices we had been scanning and made a comparison before making a decision from them. Don't you think?', he asked her rhetorically.

'I don't know. You and mum can decide', she returned an educated answer as they slowly exit the car yard.

They tried again the following weekend to purchase a car and they eventually found one that can fit them all and consequently bought it. It was not as flashy as the company car he used as an industrial radiographer but modest enough to start off with. It was another step forward for them.

The Australian Recipe

Timbo had four children already, all girls. After their second child, they decided to give it a break before trying again for a boy. But when they tried six years later a twin girls arrived. They were not disappointed with their expectation but overjoyed. It was the first set of twins in their immediate families. It was only after some time that Timbo found out their twin girls was the twelfth set of twins in the family.

Despite being blessed with them he still yearned for a son. He had been talking to several friends and been told various myths in getting a boy. One of which was from his work colleague. She told him some non-scientific belief that if the mother refrained from dairy products in the first trimester, the chance of getting a boy is very high. She tried it herself and it worked.

'I'll ask my wife if she can manage going without milk and butter the next time', Timbo jokingly accepted.

When he got home his wife questioned his joyous mood.

'I have some news dear', he announced.

'*Good or bad?',* she questioned.

'I dont know'.

'What do you mean you don't know?', she prompted him.

'If it comes in your favour then it's good news, if not, bad luck', he kept her in wonder.

'But what is it?'

'I don't know if you can manage it'.

'Well, if you do not want to tell me now, you may as well forget it', she seemed to lose her eagerness.

'I was talking to one of my colleagues about a baby boy, and she said',

'Is it your colleague or your girlfriend', she humorously interrupted.

'Come on, let me finish'.

'Ok, finish your girlfriend's story', she teased him.

'Oh, you funny thing. Anyway', he tried to continue, *'she said if we try again, you should try and abstain from all dairy products in the first trimester, we might get the luck. It worked with her'.*

'So why should I try again when you've already got a son with her?', she kept teasing him as she made cups of tea for them.

'Goodness me, what are you getting at?', he commented defensively.

She returned with his cup of tea, stroked his head, *'Take that, it's my recipe'*, she laughed. *'We'll try your Australian recipe if it works. Don't forget, that's the last one'*, she facetiously acquiesced with a stop sign on it. Timbo just sipped his tea and shook his head in disbelief at his wife's humorous side.

When she conceived again, she tried very hard to abide by the 'no dairy product myth' for the sake of getting a son. Timbo too tried to alleviate her dedication by following suit. It was tough especially with something that could have been proven scientifically but not. They just adopted it as a last resort. They had already had two girls from the islands, twin girls from New Zealand; it was the Aussie turn then.

On their first visit to the doctor, they were opened to any news. They've already had twins, they would not be surprised if another one was declared. But the doctor could only hear one heartbeat. It did not stop him from sending them for ultrasound scanning for confirmation. Timbo, a medical radiographer himself, was familiar with images while his wife was being scanned. He was not only following the wellbeing of the baby, but most importantly, the outcome of the Australian recipe. To his excitement, the sonographer confirmed their dream, it's a boy.

On their way to the car, he could not contain his ecstasy, *'I told you but you tried to make fun of me'*.

'Well, your girlfriend's recipe works', she joked.

'I don't care what you say but I'm getting a son to look after the girls', he stated in relief.

The Turn of Tide

On the day of delivery, Timbo took a day off work to drive his wife to the hospital. His two older daughters skipped school as well to accompany their mother to hospital. They knew from previous appointments the hospital car parking was always full every day. Despite leaving earlier, they still had to circle twice before they could find a parking in the paid full day Parking.

After checking into the room, Timbo thought he would delay buying his children's breakfast because her appointment was 9.00am. However, it dragged on until he was not sure what to do. He was vacillating on whether or not to run for kids' food. If he sneaked out to buy something for them, that could be the time they might come and took her to theatre.

Timbo's speculation was right. It was not even five minutes after they left with the twins when the team arrived to take his wife. Upon returning, his older daughter was still waiting for them. *'What time did they take her?'*, he asked her.

'They came just after you left, maybe five minutes', she answered in tears.

'Did they say anything?'

'They said they were taking her to the theatre', she answered.

'We'll go down to the theatre waiting room and have your feed there', he told them all.

While his daughters were having their late breakfast, he went over to the patients waiting bay to see if his wife was still there. His hospital experience prompted him to meet up with her again. He was allowed in her previous operations and thus asked the charge nurse if he could be present during delivery. When given the green light, he went back to the children and told them of the change of plan; they had to stay on their own in the waiting room while he would be in theatre with their mother.

He did not think much of it. It did not cross his mind that circling for a parking and their absence when she was taken to theatre were shadows casted over coming events.

The operation started normally and it did not take long for the baby to be delivered. *'Here you are, congratulations'*, the midwife said as she handled him the baby.

'Thanks', he uttered through his mask as he joyfully accepted him. He handed him over to his wife for the first maternal kiss and view. As he took him away from her, she appeared withdrawn and fell asleep. She looked pale and lips were turning blue all of a sudden. He tried to put the oxygen mask on her but the charge nurse turned to him, *'What are doing?'*, she challenged his actions.

'She's turning blue', he timidly justified his action.

'He's a radiographer, he knows what he's doing', intervened the operating medical officer. *'Can someone call the emergency team'*, he shouted through his mask.

He turned to Timbo, *'If you don't mind, we want you to wait with the baby outside please'*, requested the Doctor. Timbo did not want to leave but it was for the sake of his wife he had to leave. He whispered her ear, *'I love you dear, the kids are sending their love too; we'll see you outside'*. She was not responding then but he left with all his faith in the doctors' ingenuity that things would turn out favourably.

Once he met up with his daughters again, they came crowding curiously around to cuddle and kiss their brother. They all wanted to cuddle and thus took turns to hold him. They were all excited but Timbo was worried and confused. *'How is mum?'* they started asking.

'She's ok, she'll be out soon', he calmly answered them.

After two hours of waiting, one of the doctors came out to see them. Timbo started sensing trouble based on the doctor's worried appearance.

'*Hi, I'm Dr Viro, I'm here to keep you update on your wife's progress. We are still working hard to stop the bleeding which is why it's taking a bit longer for her to be out*', she tried to explain the situation. '*Do you have anyone to call?. You can call them. I'm not quite sure of how long. Things are not looking good but we are trying our best. Do you want to go home and have a rest and we'll call you after?*' she asked sympathetically.

'*No, it's ok. We can wait*', Timbo responded anxiously while holding onto his new born son.

'*Alright, I'll keep you informed*', she agreed.

The children were still cuddling their brother and listened but not aware of the problem. '*What was she talking about?*' his eldest daughter tried to make sense of the doctors call.

'*She said they are still working hard to make our wait shorter*', Timbo answered calmly.

'*Why, is mum alright?*' she seemed to be aware of the doctor's visit.

'*When they complete their job without doubt, she will be alright*', he tried to pacify them all.

'*But why did she mention phone call?*'

'*It's an alternative option to make our relatives and friends aware of our situation?*'.

'*Why should they know?*'

'*Moral support my dear?*' he was surprised at how curious she was in bombarding him with all these questions.

'*Will you call any one?*' she kept going.

'*I'm not really keen to at the moment but if it takes a bit longer I'll probably call your uncle Paul who is close by, then my mum in Hawaii*'.

After a while, Timbo finally decided to make a phone call. He tried his brother Paul first but after the second unsuccessful attempt he tried his mother in Hawaii.

'*Hello*', it was his sister's voice

149

'Hello, its Timbo', was Timbo's controlled voice

'Hi Timbo, It's nice to hear you again. It's been a while since I haven't heard your voice. How are you and the family?', was his sister's excited voice.

'Ok, nice to hear you too. How's mum?'

'She's good. She's here. Wait, let me give her the phone'.

'Hello Timbo', his mum answered excitedly.

'Hi mum. How are you?'

'I'm very strong and healthy', she jokingly answered.

'How about you and the family? When is the baby due?' she added.

'We are Ok. Ira and Martha are holding onto their brother now; he's only three hours old now and he's fine'.

'Oh congratulations, very nice to hear you finally have a son. So how's his mother?'.

'That's why I'm calling. The baby is fine but his mother is still in theatre.'

'Why? What happened?', his mother interrupted.

'It's been three hours now since the baby's out', Timbo continued. 'We've been told things are not looking good for her and to call anyone we want to call. That's why I'm calling to make you aware in case of any unwanted outcome'.

Timbo could hear heavy breathing from his mother but she did not say a thing.

When she spoke again, the excitement had gone but she was trying to say some comforting word to Timbo. He was still content in holding his cool to calm his mother. His sister broke in to save time and money on phone bill, 'Have you called Paul?' she queried

'I've tried but he's not home. I'll try again after talking to you.'

'Mum's crying but our hearts are with you, your kids and your wife in particular. She's done a lot for us especially our mum. That's why mum's so distressed. Try Paul again and we'll call him too. But be strong for the kids'.

Before she hung up, '*Here's mum again. We'll talk again. Bye Timbo*', cracked her sister's voice.

'*Timbo*', his mum's voice trembled through, '*send my love to your wife. Lets all save our prayers for her*'.

Seeing the doctor coming again he had to cut short their conversation. The doctor's face told it all. She looked very distraught and uncomfortable.

'*Hi, it's good that you are talking to someone. We are still working on her, but...*', she paused, took a deep breath and continued, '*but it will be for a while*'. In a very calm voice, '*You've had a long day, especially the kids. We suggest its best you go home and feed them and have a rest; we will call you when she's out. Is that ok with you?*'.

Timbo nodded. He was about to query the baby's destination when she said, '*A nurse will come with a cot for the baby and take him to the nursery and you can visit him anytime*'.

'*We'll do that. Many thanks for the update and advice*', he agreed.

It was late in the afternoon since they left the house early dawn. The children were obviously exhausted and hungry. He was more concerned with his wife's operation and their children's future wellbeing should any unwanted consequences arose.

They met Paul on their way home and he followed them. Their mother must have called him. They were still cooking some food when the hospital called again.

'*Hello its Timbo*'.

'*Hi Timbo, I'm the one talking to you when you were in hospital. How are you?*', the doctor introduced himself again.

'*I'm fine thanks*', Timbo tried to be calm while answering.

'*Good. It's good that you've got the children home to have some rest. Your wife is out of theatre and she is now in the Intensive Care Unit. We are closely observing her at this time and will call you again if we need to do anything more*'.

'*Many thanks indeed, it's very much appreciated*', he applauded her call with great relief.

His relief didn't last long. They were about to start their dinner when the phone rang again. *'Hello, its Timbo'*, he answered unwittingly.

'Hi Timbo, it's me again. Sorry to bother you. Your wife is still bleeding and that's why I'm calling again if you can come in again to sign the consent form so we can take her back again to theatre to rectify the problem before it's too late', she informed him.

'Thanks for the call. That's no problem I shall be there as soon as I can', he offered enthusiastically but scared of the unwanted outcome. He sacrificed his meal and calmly put the children at ease in the care of his sister in law before rushing back to the hospital with his brother.

His brother was trying to crack the conversation on the way over but Timbo was still lost for words at such a time.

Arriving at the hospital, Timbo was shocked at how much his wife's body was swelling. He whispered into her ear to hold his hand if she could hear him but there was no response. He was terrified. He had seen many seriously ill patients before in the course of his service but this was the worst one, his wife. She was definitely in a very critical condition. His heart froze. He was a bit confident during the day but as the night got darker and darker and so was his hope. The emptiness he was starting to see appeared endless and inexplicable. His brother's presence helped but did not ease his discomfort or his uneasiness.

After signing the *Consent Form*, the consultant specialist who would do the operation got hold of Timbo and took him aside, *'I'm Dr Bubla, I'll be doing the operation. It's good that you are here to witness her condition. As you can see there is very little chance we can turn things around. But we will try our best'*, he briefed Timbo privately. Timbo thanked him stoically.

As they pushed her to the theatre at midnight, the charge nurse sang out, *'Do you believe in God?'*.

'Yes', Timbo mumbled back.

'Pray for a miracle', she appealed to him as they disappeared to the theatre.

Timbo was lost in thoughts and words. When his brother pleaded with him to make some phone calls to whoever they could contact to be aware of the unexpected, Timbo was undecided. He still had a strong conviction that she would pull through all the odds. It was only after they had been waiting for more than two hours that he finally gave in to his brother's insistence to call their mother in particular.

Upon calling her, she was quick to pick up the phone and asked for an update. Timbo's brother gave her an update but Timbo was too distraught to talk to anyone then and thus, his brother hung up without passing the phone to Timbo.

It was the longest night in Timbo's life. Their priest and wife turned up unexpectedly in the waiting room. They started straightaway with a prayer before greeting each other. It was more or less a prayer night interspersed briefly with some counselling words from the priest.

Whenever they heard footsteps coming their way, they would all stop talking, held their breaths and waited if it's for them or not. They would only resume their brief talks or prayers when the noise faded away from. They were also indifferent to anyone entering their privacy at such time. No one was prepared to receive any unwanted news.

At six o'clock in the morning, they heard shoes coming straight to them; it was the consultant doctor performing the operation. He was still in blue operating theatre gown, *'Good morning'*, he greeted them.

'Good morning sir', they returned the greeting in a very nervous mood.

'Your prayers are answered', he declared. *'We've managed to stop the bleeding but we'll keep a close eye on her in the first forty eight hours for any likely reactions to donors' blood she is now thriving on. She has lost a lot of blood. It is therefore very important to restrict visitation within that period of time to avoid infection. Otherwise she will be fine after that time frame'*, he clarified the situation.

'Are there any questions?'

'No sir excepting that we are very grateful to you and the team for the hard job done', Timbo said emotionally.

'It's a pleasure and thanks for the prayers too', he cheered them up. He wanted to make sure they understood what he explained before he left. But all doubts had been succumbed by the success story of the operation. *'I'll see you later'*, he gave a cheering gesture and left.

There was loud talk of cheerfulness in the waiting room after the doctor left; it was a big sigh of relief. It was a whole night of prayers; a feat that was finally paid off, their prayers were answered. The news was followed by a very long prayer of thanksgiving.

Timbo's brother was on the phone again to relay the good news to their waiting mother.

The church minister offered his final counseling before returning home to prepare for the Sunday Mass. Timbo was emotional when thanking the priest and his wife for the thoughts in spending the night with them in hospital for his wife. The priest too was more than happy his prayers had been answered.

On the other hand, Timbo's prayer was also answered. On the Sunday following his wife's delivery, there was a youth combined service in which each youth group had to perform an item. Timbo was leading their youth group then. When it was their group's turn, Timbo danced his way up to the music as he led his group up the stage.

The crowd were cheering and clapping loudly as he toyed around the group. He went on dancing fervently as if in a dancing hall until his group was all in an organized formation on stage. But this was the Sunday where they conservatively forbid any dancing.

Thus, when his wife's delivery did not go smoothly, he quickly remembered his dancing not only on the Sunday but also in the church.

While the priest was praying for the health of Timbo's wife, Timbo was trying to justify his dancing by praying, *'Lord do not allow any unwanted ending to my wife, because I will be blamed for dancing in your church on Sunday. Please do not let me down by proving their point. But prove them that you accept people who worship you in happiness, amen'.*

While the priest was happy with the outcome of their prayers, Timbo was more than happy that he was proven right. Whoever's prayer was answered did not matter much then, Timbo's wife had been saved.

This was very impressive and memorable to Timbo. His heart went for the medical team who saved his wife. He was very overwhelmed with their sacrifices to leave whatever they were doing at home and converged at the theatre for the sake of his wife. He wished he could pay them to return the favour but did not have the money. He thought then that his only other option was to look for a job in the same hospital where he could work as a token of appreciation for their services well done.

Whether or not it would happen was a dream of his life. Only time would tell.

The Dark Radiographer

While Timbo's wife recovered in the hospital, Timbo and the children only visited when allowed. During visiting hours they avoided visiting her because of the doctor's warning. However, this would be the first time they would visit the baby since leaving him on the first night.

The baby was yet unnamed and was still in the nursery attended only by the nurses since the delivery. That was the last time they cuddled him while the operation was at its prime. He was probably wondering where his family was.

Timbo's wife was awake by the end of the day and heard everything that was going on around her but could not open her eyes because of the anesthetic aftermath.

With her long ears, she heard the nurse asking the doctor, '*Her husband wants to come in to see her, is that ok with you?*', the rostered nurse asked the medical officer on duty.

'*Is that the dark radiographer?*', Timbo's wife overhead them giggling but kept still as if she could not hear a thing.

'*Let him wait until you're ready*', was the response she heard.

'*What about her?*', queried the nurse.

'*Give her something to relieve her pain until I see her tomorrow*'.

Timbo's wife kept still with eyes still closed since double operation. She did not want to move to avoid them knowing she heard their comments.

When Timbo turned up again during visiting hours, he was at a loss why his wife cried relentlessly while holding his hand tightly. She was still in mask and tubes and Timbo tried to wipe her tears and calm her down.

'What's the matter?'. Are you alright?', Timbo asked curiously. He was worried over the reason for her crying. 'Are you alright?', he insisted. She just nodded. She tried to say something but Timbo was still in the dark; he could not comprehend what she was trying to say because of the mask and tubes connected to it.

When she calmed down, she told Timbo of what she overhead, especially calling him a 'Dark Radiographer'.

'Don't worry dear, as long as you recover, that's the main thing', comforted Timbo.

The following day, she was free of tubes and the many lines she was connected to. By the end of the week, she was fully recovered. On Saturday morning after breakfast, a nun turned up unexpectedly, 'Can I come in?', she asked Timbo's wife.

'Sure'.

'I'm Sister Mary visiting every patient in the hospital', she introduced herself. 'I heard you are the miracle lady surviving all the odds', she continued.

'Thank you', Timbo's wife returned with a smile.

'We can only be thankful for the Divine support for chances we've been given. That's why I'm here, to pray for you. Shall we pray?', she asked and prayed straightaway.

After the prayer the nun wished Timbo's wife good health and left. Two hours later, the medical officer in charge gave a final checking for Timbo's wife before discharging.

Timbo was very relieved and grateful to the medical care she was given. Thus, he was determined to apply for a radiographic post in the same hospital to reciprocate their service.

It took a fair while for her to recover fully. Amazingly, she was given home assistance service until she recovered. The hospital arranged for it before discharging her and it was a great help to the family as his wife concentrated on getting better and as their household adjusted to having a baby in the house.

Timbo and his wife treasured the home service highly because it gave him the chance to resume working while she was cared for by such team until she fully recovered. They did not know such a service existed and were very grateful for it.

The Reciprocal Dream

When Timbo saw an ad for a job in the same hospital his son was born in, he did not hesitate but went for it. One of the key questions he was asked, *'Why are you applying for this job when you've got one already closer to you?'*

'My wife had a baby here and almost did not make it through. I was and still am astounded with the effort of the team that saved her from her operation. I did not have the money to pay them for such a sacrifice but if I get this one, it would be a golden opportunity to reciprocate through other patients', he openly admitted.

The interview had gone well and Timbo was offered the job, and he could not be more contented. It did not matter much to him whether or not it was his declaration during the interview that got him over the line. All he had to do then was to fulfill his promise at whatever time his service was requested.

When called to work one night, he almost flipped his car when negotiating the intersection. The day was raining and he underestimated the road's elusive slippery condition such that the car swerved 180 degrees. Luckily, there was no other car in front or behind him or even a pedestrian nearby.

Timbo was obviously shocked at the unexpected incident. He stopped briefly to breathe before continuing at a speed slower than before. His experience with his wife's delivery complications reminded him of the importance of prompt response and the consequent attendance. He also knew that he needed to proceed cautiously in order to help.

Arriving safely at work, Timbo went to the operating theatre where the patient and team were still waiting patiently for him. He tried to offer his apology for keeping them waiting but they just accepted his apology graciously which alleviated his uneasiness.

Timbo was glad he had finally achieved his dream of returning the favour not in monetary form but through his service. He had been pursuing his various goals and seen many places through various forms of sponsorships. But this was the most decisive time of his life.

His decision to make a full commitment to serve others would help him help others like what they had done to him financially and professionally through sponsorships, scholarships and service, and lately to his wife.

He could not be more relaxed and happier. Despite the technological changes since starting his career, Timbo was still anxious to evolve with them and be productive to those in need of them. It would only be then that he would consider his life helpful if not useful in service to the public as he vowed to give in return.

He had been through many phases of humanity. He had witnessed the many changes in technology that affect many aspects of life. He had also seen both sides of the coin in the way we live; some enjoying while others yearned to survive from one day to the other. But nothing changed the continuous effort of the many kind souls in trying to make the unfortunate lives meaningful and our world a peaceful and enjoyable place to live.

Epilogue

The sun was on the horizon and the breeze kept fanning Timbo while he enjoyed the swing of his hammock. He was still admiring the birds making their last lark, as a call of thanks, as they started leaving their feed one by one. It reminded him of the echo of the coconut and the ripe banana that started his life.

He could not get over the life he had. He treasured every moment he had with special thanks to his sponsors, locally and abroad, who opened the doors for him in the various institutes and in different circumstances. Without them, his vision of the world would still be like the sun in the hut.

There had been bumps on the way Timbo reflected, but without them he would still be a radiographer in the dark not seeing the meaning of humanity through the kind-heartedness of the fortunate to the unfortunate ones, let alone the divine providence. He cherished them all and saluted them unreservedly.

His thoughts went to his parents and their dedication to improving their children's lot in life. Despite the hardship in turning land products into cash for him and his siblings, they were now each successful in their own right.

Now that he has seen most of the world, in reality and through the media, he could not be any selfish to deny others the same life he yearned for, especially his children who may never see the joy of cuddling the coconut for the sake of getting a prospective life.

Thanks for reading.

God Bless.

www.ingramcontent.com/pod-product-compliance
Lightning Source LLC
Chambersburg PA
CBHW070012140726
47908CB00020B/1271